WHEN NIGHT FALLS

Kaitlyn O'Connor

Futuristic Romance

New Concepts   Georgia

Kaitlyn O'Connor

Be sure to check out our website for the very best in fiction at fantastic prices!

When you visit our webpage, you can:

* Read excerpts of currently available books
* View cover art of upcoming books and current releases
* Find out more about the talented artists who capture the magic of the writer's imagination on the covers
* Order books from our backlist
* Find out the latest NCP and author news--including any upcoming book signings by your favorite NCP author
* Read author bios and reviews of our books
* Get NCP submission guidelines
* And so much more!

We offer a 20% discount on all new ebook releases!
(Sorry, but short stories are not included in this offer.)

We also have contests and sales regularly, so be sure to visit our webpage to find the best deals in ebooks and paperbacks! To find out about our new releases as soon as they are available, please be sure to sign up for our newsletter (http://www.newconceptspublishing.com/newsletter.htm) or join our reader group (http://groups.yahoo.com/group/new_concepts_pub/join) !

The newsletter is available by double opt in only and our customer information is *never* shared!

Visit our webpage at:
www.newconceptspublishing.com

When Night Falls is an original publication of NCP. This work has never before appeared in book form. This work is a novel. Any similarity to actual persons or events is purely coincidental.

New Concepts Publishing
5202 Humphreys Rd.
Lake Park, GA 31636

ISBN 1-58608-685-5
© copyright 2004 Kaitlyn O'Connor
Cover art by Jenny Dixon, © copyright 2004

NCP books are available at special quantity discounts for bulk purchases for sales promotions, premiums, fund raising, or educational use. For details, write, email, or phone New Concepts Publishing, 5202Humphreys Rd., Lake Park, GA 31636, ncp@newconceptspublishing.com, Ph. 229-257-0367, Fax 229-219-1097.

First NCP Paperback Printing: 2005

Printed in the United States of America

Other Titles from NCP by Kaitlyn O'Connor:

The Lion's Woman (Now in Trade Paperback)
The Claiming
Below
Guardian of the Storm
Abiogenesis (Now in Trade Paperback)
Exiled
Cyborg

Chapter One

The planet below them looked surprisingly beautiful considering that it was a dead world. Dr. Tessa Bergin studied its surface with a mixture of frustration and disgust. Strictly speaking, it was not actually dead, but the civilization they had traveled so far to contact was.

Two years ago, when they had left Earth, she had been filled with excitement to be a part of the mission that would contact the advanced civilization their deep space probes had discovered. From all indications, it was at least their equal, and very likely even more medically and technologically advanced. She had expected to learn so much from them! She had been so thrilled to escape the abject boredom of the museum she worked in and the endless rounds of restoring and studying the same stale artifacts that never seemed to actually lead anywhere.

Finally, she would get the chance to discover things on her own! Finally, she would not have to do the drudge work of the more experienced scientists!

Half way out, they had woken from their fourth deep sleep cycle to the discovery that something had gone terribly wrong. While they had slept, an entire world of people had died, taking their civilization with them.

Instead of setting down and negotiating a working relationship with another race, they would be studying the remains of the civilization that had vanished, virtually overnight.

She would be fortunate if they even allowed her to set foot on the planet! Anthropology was her field, but there was certainly no urgency to study the civilization now--dead was dead. She could only dig and speculate and try to figure out what sort of civilization had been there, if she was allowed to go. She wouldn't get the chance to study a working, vital, social structure that was completely different from their own.

Tessa frowned. Whatever it was that had devastated this world, it did not seem to have been war--which certainly supported the theory of an advanced race. They had not found traces of a geological disaster, either natural or the result of poor conservation. The atmosphere was clear--amazingly so actually considering the estimated size of the population that had once inhabited the world. But then, they had calculated that at least ten years and possibly as much as fifteen to twenty, Earth time, had passed since the disaster. If the devastation was the result of a global cataclysm, there had been plenty of time for the planet to stabilize.

It was the one thing about deep space travel that had unnerved her about volunteering to make the trip--the effect time travel had on time. Not that it made that much difference to her, she supposed. She'd left no one behind--no one on the mission had. It was one of the requisites, that they have no close family ties, and probably the only reason she'd been allowed to fill a slot. It was just too traumatic for those who took the deep space missions to return and discover so many years had passed in their absence, that their children had grown up, their parents died, their spouse had grown old--two years out and already ten to twenty years had passed on Earth, despite the speed they were traveling. By the time they got back, most everyone they'd known and worked with would have died.

Her irritation resurfaced. She'd given up the world she'd known just for the chance of discovery, and now it seemed she'd given it up for nothing!

She pushed the thought aside as Dr. Boyd came to stand beside her. He was a tall man but bent slightly now with age. Despite that, he had a kindly look about him and he wasn't nearly as testy as most of his colleagues. "Were you picked for the first landing?"

"No," she said, trying not to sound sullen even though his obvious excitement exacerbated her feelings of ill usage.

He scrubbed his hands together almost gleefully. "I'll be going."

Tessa resisted the urge to roll her eyes. As *if* she couldn't have guessed! "No! Really? Well, congratulations, Dr. Boyd."

He turned to grin at her, as excited as kid, although he was probably sixty if he was a day, maybe older. He joined them from the CDC--his job, naturally enough, to make certain they didn't pick up any deadly diseases to take home with them.

In fact, except for herself and Dr. Layla Lehman (or LayLeh as most everybody called her), who was only four years her senior, the majority of the scientists aboard the *Meadowlark* were middle aged or older.

It was one of the reasons, she knew, that her opinion wasn't precisely respected, despite her degree, despite the years she'd spent paying her 'dues'--she was still under thirty and not seasoned enough.

The other, of course, was because she hadn't done

any field work.

It began to seem unlikely that this was going to be her chance for it.

Shaking her irritation, Tessa left Dr. Boyd at the observation window and made her way down to the lab to study the read outs from the probes. The atmosphere was a reassuring balance of oxygen, hydrogen, etc., etc.--probably better than the air they breathed on Earth despite the numerous scrubbers that had been built to help to purify Earth's air. She couldn't see that the planet, dubbed PIM9162 after their probes had discovered it in the Claxton Galaxy--a galaxy previous believed to have no livable planets--had changed radically from the pre-disaster period.

The bacteria identified through earlier probes had not changed significantly either--certainly not enough to indicate that it might have had anything to do with the devastation, but, as far as they'd been able to determine, *something* had reduced the dominant species on the planet by approximately ninety percent ten to fifteen planet years earlier.

There were survivors, or at least there had been as far as they could tell, but very likely finding the scattered remains of the race would prove to be difficult, and what were the odds that, even if they did, it would turn out to be scientists?

She wasn't interested in the mathematical probability anyway.

Despite her disappointment, and her envy of those who would be allowed to be among the first to land on the surface of the planet, Tessa found she couldn't resist going down to the docking bay to see the landing crew off when they began preparing for the first launch.

Layleh was among those who would be going down. The two of them had become friends since they'd left Earth, despite the fact that they actually had very little in common. Layleh was a linguist. As intelligent as she was, she had the sort of sparkling personality that made her seem more of a social butterfly than a serious scientist--and it was that that had initially put Tessa off--that and the fact that she had a rapier wit and a tongue to match and could run circles around pretty much anyone who was unwise enough to match 'swords' with her--especially Tessa, who was more inclined to spill her guts the moment a thought occurred to her than to consider before she spoke.

She liked Layleh best when she was giving one of the other scientists onboard a hard time.

"Tessa!"

Tessa smiled as Layleh danced over to her and gave her a hug. Layleh's eyes were twinkling when she pulled away. "I thought sure you'd be in your cabin enjoying your misery and refuse to see me off."

Tessa's smile turned wry. "That obvious, huh?"

Layleh chuckled. "Don't worry. Only to me. The others are like kids at Christmas ... and not terribly observant of others at the best of times." She sighed. "Self absorbed doesn't even begin to describe this bunch. If it wasn't ingrained habit with them to dress when they got out of bed, I suspect half of them would be walking around in the buff most of the time."

Tessa gave her a searching look. "You're not ... the least bit anxious?"

Layleh bit her lip wryly. "Scared shitless! But I'm excited, too. Of course fate--or the law of averages--

being what it is, the chances are my services won't even be necessary and I'll be stuck watching the lander, or something equally boring, while everyone else runs around making exciting discoveries."

Tessa gave her a sympathetic look.

"Of course," Layleh said thoughtfully, "there's always the possibility that I might be swept off my feet by some gorgeous alien male!"

Tessa couldn't help but chuckle, even though she was more than a little horrified by Layleh's preoccupation with the opposite sex. "You do realize we don't know what the dominant species of this world is like--other than that they appear to be intellectually advanced? They could look like--lizards for all we know--or something even less appealing. And it's very doubtful that we would be sexually compatible."

Layleh leaned close. "After two years on this tub with fifteen fifty to seventy year old men--scientists who probably weren't even exciting when they were young, *if* they were ever young--if they've got the right kind of equipment down below, they'll look good. And I'm willing to try anything at least once."

"Serious--oh, you're joking!"

Layleh's smile vanished. "Not altogether," she said wryly. "I hate to admit it, but even the droid crew is starting to look good to me. I've worn my toys out and what're the odds, you think, that they'll have more here? Anyway, I could always close my eyes and think good thoughts," she added, grinning.

Tessa felt a deep red blush climb all the way to her hairline. "Layleh! You can't expect to be taken seriously as a scientist if all you ever think about is sex!"

Layleh's brows rose, but her eyes twinkled with repressed laughter. "That's not true! I think about other things."

"Like what?" Tessa asked suspiciously.

Layleh chuckled. "Men."

Tessa gaped at her. Layleh patted the bottom of her chin, lifting her sagging jaw, and then patted her cheek. "You take everything too seriously, Tessa! You've only got one life. Live it, for god's sake! Enjoy what you can--and try to see if you can lose that guilt complex you carry around everywhere you go. You spend way too much time around moldy things."

Tessa smiled with an effort. "I was hoping I'd get the chance to study something a little 'fresher' on this trip."

Layleh hugged her again. "You will--see you in a few days."

She waved back when Layleh strode up the gang plank and paused to wave jauntily at her, but inwardly she didn't feel the least bit unconcerned about the expedition. Layleh might be right. Maybe she did take things much too seriously, but Layleh didn't seem to take anything seriously enough. There was no telling what sort of dangers they might be facing, and yet Layleh acted as if she was going on a … lark without a care in the world.

She didn't see Layleh in a few day's time. They had one communication from the group as they made several passes over the city they'd chosen, describing what they could see from the air. The group checked in as they reached the landing site and began their final landing preparations. After that, they heard nothing. The landing party ceased to communicate with the mother ship and all attempts to hail them resulted in nothing but dead air.

"They're in trouble," Tessa said to the group that had gathered around the conference table two days after the group had left. "We need to organize a rescue party."

Sinclair, the head of the expedition, frowned thoughtfully. "We don't know that they're in trouble. Their communications are out. It could be anything-- equipment malfunction, adverse weather conditions, interference of some kind on the ground...."

"Hostiles?"

Sinclair glared at Tessa. "We have no reason to believe that we would be met with hostility. This is a civilized world, very likely even more advanced than our own."

"Was," Tessa corrected. "Whatever happened here broke down the entire fabric of their civilization. If there are survivors--they *are* survivors, and that means they've almost certainly had to resort to survival by might. That also means we're dealing with an extremely intelligent race that is, most likely, also barbaric now and considerably more dangerous than mere primitives would be. We should have considered the possibility that we might be met with a determination to take what we've got for their own survival, rather than a welcoming committee."

Sinclair looked around the table at the other scientists, his bushy white brows lifted questioningly. They seemed to be more or less equally divided. Half of them were considering her suggestions, the other half looked at her pretty much the way Sinclair usually did, with a mixture of condescension and amusement.

"Mathematically speaking, with a civilization as advanced as this one appears to have been, the percentile of survivors would almost certainly be made up of rational beings."

Tessa gave him a look. "Directly after the catastrophe--you're probably right. As conditions grew worse from the break down, however, 'rational' could have boiled down to who had what they needed to survive and who didn't and whether the 'haves' were strong enough to beat the 'have nots' off of it--look, I don't really see a lot of point in sitting here, miles above the planet, debating whether or not our landing party met with hostile natives. We haven't heard from them since the day they landed. They were due back yesterday. Anything could have happened to them, and I do mean anything. But we can't help them from here. We're going to have to go down and see if we can pull them out."

Sinclair glared at her. "We're scientists, not soldiers. We came to learn. We've virtually no weapons, and none of us know how to use what we do have."

"How hard can it be to point and fire?" Tessa demanded in exasperation.

His lips thinned. "You're suggesting we go down and attack anything that moves?"

"I'm not suggesting anything of the kind! I'm only saying we go armed. If it looks like the landing group was attacked and captured by hostile aliens, we do what we have to to get them back."

"Thank you for your input, Dr. Bergin," Sinclair said tightly. "We'll take it under advisement. I'd like to hear from the rest of you what your views on this are, and whether or not we should delay the second landing...."

Tessa gaped at him in disbelief for several moments and finally stormed out of the room. It was all very well to say that they'd all known that there were risks involved in taking on such a mission, but she at least, had assumed that they would watch each other's back since they couldn't count on rescue from any other quarter. She'd thought that was why they'd taken the precaution of only sending part of the scientific team down. Now, instead of immediately going to check out the danger of the landing team, Dr. Sinclair had waited until they didn't return as expected and then called a meeting.

She was waiting impatiently in front of the starboard viewing port when the meeting finally broke up and the men began to emerge. She turned to study their faces, trying to figure out what had been decided. Her stomach tightened when Sinclair emerged, glanced at her and then pointedly turned in the other direction and strode off toward his quarters. She realized then that few of the men had actually met her questioning gaze at all.

Lee Harris approached her. "They've agreed to do a fly over tomorrow."

Tessa blinked at him in shock. "Excuse me?"

He shrugged, gesturing out the viewing port. "It would be dark on the side where they landed before we could ready a lander to go down. We'll go down tomorrow and see if we can tell anything about the condition of the other lander. If it looks like it was attacked, we won't land--we're just not prepared to launch an aggressive rescue, Tessa. I'm sorry. I know you were fond of Dr. Lehman."

A wave of nausea washed over her. Were--past tense. Apparently she'd been more convincing than she'd thought. They weren't taking any chances that she might be right, but it had never occurred to her that she was convincing them *not* to go. She should've just kept her big mouth shut. "But ... they could still be alive. We can't just abandon them!"

"And they could be dead. Will it help them if we're dead too?"

She went to her quarters when he'd left, too sick at heart to feel like looking at her fellow crew members. She wanted to try reasoning with them. She wanted to scream and curse and raise total hell, but she might just as well beat her head on the bulkhead for all the good it was likely to do.

She paced the room for a while and finally flung herself down on the bunk, staring up at the ceiling. She knew, in her heart, that if it was her down there, Layla would have managed to get a rescue team together. Layla was good with people. She could always manage to talk them into doing what she wanted them to do.

She also knew that if, when they went down, they saw that the lander *had* been attacked, Sinclair would scrub the mission right then and there and turn tail for Earth.

A totally insane thought drifted through her mind.

She dismissed it, but not only would it refuse to stay banished, each time it flitted through her mind again, it grew stronger.

What could she accomplish, alone? She asked herself.

What could you accomplish if you had that pack of spineless white meat at your back? Her inner self countered.

The answer seemed inarguable. She'd be no worse off, and no less likely to be successful if she went alone.

She was either going to have to find her spine and do what she knew she should do, or figure out how she was going to live with herself when she did nothing at all but tuck her tail between her legs and run with the rest of the craven pack.

Chapter Two

Tessa realized that fear was not an emotion she'd ever truly experienced in her entire life before. She hadn't realized how absolutely insulated she had been from real life. She'd been nervous. She'd been anxious. She had even been spooked more than once, but sheer terror was a totally new and very unwelcome experience. It made her feel hot and cold at the same time, and nauseated to the point where she felt as if she would throw up ... or pass out from hyperventilation.

She'd slipped a note under Dr. Harris' door, asking him to try to keep Sinclair from abandoning them, to give her at least three days to try to find the missing party.

She knew the moment she left the docking bay, however, that she'd been lying to herself that it would make one iota's worth of difference to Sinclair. Dr. Harris might be able to convince enough of the other members to hold him off, but the likelihood was that Sinclair would bolt as soon as he discovered she'd taken the other lander.

As she dropped through the atmosphere and came nearer her destination, the direction of her terror shifted. It didn't lessen. It simply changed from fear of being abandoned to her fear of what she would face on the planet below her. If she hadn't become so fixated on her determination to try to find Layla that that thought prevailed even through the mindless state of terror that gripped her, she would probably have turned around and fled back to the ship. As it was, that option didn't even occur to her.

Gradually, the fear began to subside, burnt up by its own intensity, and her body ceased to pump adrenaline through her system in sickening, knee weakening waves. Awe pressed it a little further to the back of her mind as she broke through the thick cloud covering and was met with a brilliant red and gold sunrise. From her height, the land mass below showed signs even now of what had once been cultivated fields broken by straight lines of road that crisscrossed and went off in every direction.

The landing party had opted to land near one of the greater metropolitan areas, certain that if there *were* still survivors, they would be found near the remains of their civilization.

Apparently, they'd been right.

A stab of fresh fear went through her, but despite that, Tessa was so overawed at her first sight of the alien city that she was momentarily distracted from her fears. Like the people of Earth, as their population had grown, they'd begun to build higher instead of continuing to spread outward. Unlike Earth people, however, they'd never, apparently, lost their love for beautifying their surroundings. The buildings were already showing signs of decay, but from the oldest to the newest, each building seemed to vie to be the most graceful, the most ornate. Arches dominated most of the structures--windows and doors were round, or arched, but never square or rectangular. Ornate columns abounded, as did decorative cornices and friezes. Sculptures--like ancient gargoyles, perched on every available ledge and rooftop.

The similarity of much of the architecture to more ancient Earth creations pulled at the anthropologist in her and it was with a pang of regret for lost opportunity that she focused once more on her objective as the lander cruised past the city and dropped lower as it approached the landing area.

When she reached the coordinates the computer had used for the first landing, she didn't see the other lander. She circled, dropping a little lower with each pass. Her first thought when she finally did spot the lander was that they must have crashed--but that had to be wrong. The landing party had radioed back that they were landing. If there'd been any sort of problem with the equipment, they would've reported it then.

Nevertheless, even from her viewpoint she could see that the craft had been smashed all to hell and gone. Maybe they'd crashed when they'd tried to take off again?

She saw the first body when she directed the lander to drop and hover above the downed vehicle and her heart leapt into her throat. Stunned, even though she'd told herself that she must accept that they had been attacked or met with some other misfortune, Tessa stared at the unmoving form fixedly for some moments before her brain finally kicked in again.

More accurately, her brain was kicked into functioning when an object slammed into the side of her lander hard enough it rocked it.

"Climb!" she yelled, glancing around for any sign that the impact might be weather related even while her brain screamed 'attack'!

A face appeared in her viewing port, and then a

second and a third.

Tessa screamed instinctively at the jolt that went through her, but it was not merely that she was startled by the suddenness, or even the fact that she was still a good thirty feet from the ground.

The creatures hammering at the lander were like something out of a nightmare. Their faces and bodies were more human-like than any sort of beast, but their skin was a dark reddish brown and from their foreheads sprouted a pair of small horns.

At just about the same moment that she realized the creatures were also winged, the lander began to lose altitude--either from the sheer weight of numbers of the creatures piling on top of it or because one of the creatures had damaged something vital for flight. Fleeing from the porthole, Tessa strapped herself into a chair, fighting the belts. "Computer--evade."

"I do not understand the instructions."

"Go fast, then stop quickly. Go up, then down. Rotate the ship. See if you can sling them off, damn it!"

"I am unable to complete the command. The guidance is damaged. The ship is losing power."

Tessa uttered every curse word she'd ever heard. "Land the damn thing, then!"

"Assume crash position, please."

The lander slammed into the ground so hard it jarred every cell of her body. It did not simply stop, however. It continued to skid along the ground, bumping and grinding metal at a tooth jarring pace. Despite the shock and pain, uppermost in Tessa's mind was the fact that she'd been brought down by Hostiles. The ship had not even shuddered to a complete halt when she threw off her restraints and stumbled toward the weapons she'd collected and brought with her.

The crash had ripped holes in the lander, but she saw fairly quickly that none were large enough for the man-like creatures to fit through. Gathering the weapons up, she looked around for a solid place to plant her back so that she didn't have to worry about being attacked from behind. Settling in such a spot also meant she had no avenue of retreat, but that was pretty much a foregone conclusion anyway. The lander was not compartmentalized. It was strictly utilitarian and for the purpose of carrying passengers from the orbiting mother ship to the surface of a planet. They had not really intended to collect specimens of any size and had thought the landers would work for pretty much any situation since the seats could be removed if they needed or wanted to carry anything bulky.

Unfortunately, they'd only brought two landers and both of them were now scattered all over the surface of this twice damned planet.

She wasn't going home.

That thought jolted through her in a cold wave even as she tried to force her mind to concentrate on the moment ... and survival. She didn't delude herself for a moment that Sinclair would consider coming after her or any of the others--not that it seemed likely any of them would be in need of rescuing.

A shudder ran through her as she heard a pounding on the door of the lander and the scrape of metal from whatever it was they were using to batter at it.

Were these--creatures--the last remains of the civilization that had once thrived here? Or were they, like the ape, nothing more than humanoid seeming animals?

As much as she would've preferred to think the latter, she realized she already knew the answer. She'd caught no more than a glimpse. She'd been too shocked and frightened to really put the images together in her mind, but she'd seen the trappings of cognition--they were wearing loincloths and bearing weapons.

These were not animals that might get tired and go away to look for something easier to get. These were intelligent creatures bent on figuring out a way to get to her.

Dismissing it for the moment, she checked the weapons to make certain all were loaded and ready to fire. She knew very little about weapons--as Sinclair had pointed out--but she did know where the trigger was. She knew which end was the business end and she could read the display that told her it was fully loaded and ready to fire. She only had three, however, and she had no idea whether they were powerful enough to kill a full grown man--or man sized being.

She was very much afraid that she was about to find out.

They'd begun hammering on the portholes and on the hull where the crash had already weakened the structure. She shifted her position so that she could keep an eye on every place she could hear them trying to get in, wondering what they thought they'd find when they did.

Food?

She felt a wave of nausea at that thought. She was the only thing onboard that could be considered edible.

She'd seen Dr. Boyd's body, though.

Undoubtedly their goal was merely to scavenge the

lander for anything useful.

She hoped that was all they had in mind.

She frowned, trying to visualize how many were outside. She'd seen four heads at the portal, but she could recall that she'd heard the pounding on other areas at the same time. Maybe a dozen?

She checked the weapon in her lap. It had twenty four rounds. If she was right, she had enough to put several holes in each--assuming she could hit them at all--and she felt a little upsurge of hopefulness. Unless they managed to pry the door open, they'd most likely only be able to attack one at the time. Even if they did manage to pry the door open, it wasn't big enough for more than two to pass through at the time.

They were big.

A shiver ran through her as the image of their faces flashed in her mind again. There was something about them that felt threatening that went well beyond the attack itself. She allowed her mind to pick at the puzzle while she waited.

When enlightenment dawned, a cold shiver raced over her.

They looked like images she'd seen in ancient texts.

They were the human concept of evil in fleshly form--the image of the beast one of Earth's ancient myth's had called Satan.

They'd been to Earth!

Chapter Three

Tessa fired four rounds at the first one to tear the hull away enough to poke his head through. All she actually accomplished, however, was to put four more holes in the hull with the laser blasts. It took a conscious effort to stop firing when he ducked out of sight once more. The urge to simply hold the trigger down and keep firing until she'd emptied the weapon was nearly insurmountable.

She caved in to that impulse when they started hacking at the hole with a metal blade of some kind. Outside she heard several screams of pain and a good deal of scrambling as they fell back to look for cover. Encouraged, she scrambled to her feet and peered out one of the smaller holes. Two lay on the ground, writhing in pain. She saw three as they rounded a mound of debris from some building that had fallen in--perhaps demolished by her lander.

Something heavy landed on the top of the ship. She heard a roar of fury and a blade like the one she'd seen before was stabbed through, missing her by inches. Aiming upward, she peppered the top of the craft with a half dozen more holes before she heard a thud and then a sliding noise followed by a meaty thud as the creature hit the ground.

Shaking, she skittered back to her original position, huddling into as tight a ball as she could.

They didn't seem to have any weapons beyond the

blades, but those were terrifying. She'd almost rather be hit by a laser than be hacked up with something like that.

Swords. Without technology, they'd reverted to carrying swords they'd made from scavenged metal--primitive but effective, especially considering the fact that they had the strength to swing them hard enough to penetrate the hull of the lander.

She checked her perimeter, and then gauged the distance of her body from the hull. Deciding she was close enough to be in range if they figured out her position, she put a little more distance between herself and the outer wall.

She'd wounded at least three--maybe mortally, maybe not. For all she knew, the three she'd actually managed to hit might still be able to get up and come after her again--and she'd already used almost an entire power clip.

She rested, trying to calm herself, listening.

It was too much to hope they'd give up and leave.

She'd probably only managed to totally piss them off.

She was thirsty. It was warm in the lander now that it was full of holes and getting warmer. She'd panted until she'd dehydrated herself. Finally, she moved cautiously to the pack of supplies she'd brought, grabbed it and scurried back to her position. The flask of water she'd brought would hold her maybe two days--maybe. She hadn't considered that she might be pinned down and unable to get to a water supply. She'd only thought she might have trouble locating one.

After taking a couple of sips, she tightened the lid and put the flask away.

The second attack came just as she was beginning to relax.

She'd spent the time while she was waiting lecturing herself about using her ammunition wisely, but it was a thing more easily said than done. When they began pounding on the hull again from every direction, stabbing through it over and over, she emptied the pistol she had and grabbed another, firing in the direction of each sound until they once again withdrew.

Peering through the holes to watch their retreat, she saw that a couple were limping or holding an arm or their side. She'd arrived at what she thought was a fairly accurate count of her attackers, however, and she knew that she hadn't managed even to completely incapacitate half of them.

Hours passed before they launched another attack. Tessa had fired four rounds before she realized that they were throwing things toward the hull and were no where near it themselves.

"Shit!"

They knew she was scared to death. All they had to do was to keep chipping away at her nerves and she would use up every bit of ammunition she had.

Of course, they had no idea of how many weapons she had, but time was on their side. They knew that whatever she had was all she had and she'd eventually run out.

When the next wave came, she gripped the pistol and listened. Realizing they were once more bombarding the lander with debris, she held her fire.

If she'd actually been able to shoot worth a shit, she would've gone to one of the holes and tried to pick them off when they stood up to throw.

Some of the stones sounded really heavy, however, and she decided to move to a position where she could look out and see if any of them had approached close enough that she might have a chance of hitting one.

She discovered then that they were flying over and dropping the stones. She caught one of the bombers in the shoulder and watched with a mixture of satisfaction and vague nausea as he faltered and crashed to the ground.

Eventually, it became suffocatingly hot in the lander with the sun beating down on the metal, but as the day wore on she began to realize that her situation was only going to get worse when it grew too dark for her to see her attackers. Not that that looked to be the worst of her worries. At the rate she was going, she wasn't going to have any ammunition left by then anyway.

She examined the holes, wondering if there was any possibility that she might squeeze out of one of them once it got dark and make an escape. It seemed doubtful, unless they worked on the holes a lot more between now than then. She wasn't a big woman, but she wasn't tiny ... certainly not tiny enough to squeeze her ass through any of the holes currently available.

Finally, she forced herself to simply set the last weapon down. If she was holding it, she couldn't seem to stop herself from firing, instinctively, at each new threat. Setting it within easy reach, she clasped her cold hands together and tried to get her mind on something else, resolving not to touch it again until they broke through. She had enough left, maybe, to take most of them down at close range, but it was

going to have to be close. She'd already proven to
herself and to them that she couldn't even hit anything
that was standing still unless it was within a few feet of
her.

Near dusk, when they'd already launched several
assaults that went unchallenged, they came at her with
an absolute determination to break in. Tessa placed her
hand on the pistol. It was still lighter outside than
inside, and she could see their progress well enough to
know that they'd be inside with her in a matter of
minutes. Still, she waited, trying to fight the sheer
terror down and find the control she needed to survive.
They were going to have to be inside--with her. It was
the only chance she had.

She screamed when the first one climbed through,
snatching the pistol off the floor beside her and firing
two rounds at him. He fell, but there was another
directly behind him. Realizing instantly that his only
chance was to rush her, he leapt at her. She hit him
four times before she realized that it was only his
momentum that kept him heading in her direction.

Cursing, she whirled to fire at next one to enter the
lander, missing him as he ducked back outside.

The adrenaline pumping through her by now had
created havoc with her logic. She raced toward the
opening, firing again.

When she reached the opening, she saw that it looked
as if the creatures had begun to fight among
themselves. A new one that she hadn't noticed before
dropped to the ground between two of the others. The
main reason she was certain she hadn't seen him
before was because he didn't look scruffy and dirty
like the others. He was also noticeably taller than most

of them, lean, but still well muscled, his hair a deep, glossy black. He clove the head from one's shoulders even as his feet hit the dirt, whirling almost in the same motion to strike at the other man beside him. One of the creatures nearer the ship raced to take the place of the man that had been killed, his sword raised above his head like an ax. At his roar of rage, the 'dark one' shoved his opponent into the man's path. While the 'roarer' was busy trying to pull his blade out of the man he'd killed, the 'dark one' skewered him. Two other challengers raced toward him, and he began hacking at first one and then the other, whirling between them to meet their counter thrusts, twisting and finally leaping straight up as the two swung in concert--and met each other instead of him.

Dragging her gaze from the battle, she saw that there were three on the ground, unmoving. That meant there were at least four or five others besides the newest one. Her gaze was drawn to the newcomer again, but as she watched the deadly dance in front of her, something hit the top of the lander. Before she could move, her hair was seized and she was dragged up through the hole she'd been peering out of. Ignoring the painful pull on her scalp, she twisted, firing upward blindly twice before the pistol was knocked from her hand. She quickly realized she'd managed to wound the one who'd grabbed her, however. He swayed and began to topple off the top of the lander, dragging her with him.

She hit the ground so hard it knocked the breath from her. Before she could recover, two of them fell upon her, grabbing her arms and legs, clawing at her clothes. Within moments, they'd stripped her flight suit from her body and were tearing at her underclothes. She screamed again, kicking, swinging at them, biting any body part that came close enough to sink her teeth into it. Something heavy slammed into the two men she was struggling with, knocking the breath from her, but she found herself momentarily freed. Rolling over, she looked around dazedly for the pistol she'd dropped. Finally, she saw it near the hull of the ship.

Scrambling on her hands and knees, she made a dive for it, but an arm locked around her legs, slamming her to the ground once more. Wiggling, she managed to get one foot free and stomped the creature in the face. When his grip loosened, she heaved herself forward again, grabbing for the pistol . Her fingers grazed it. Before she could wrap her fingers around the grip, she was caught once more and dragged back. Rolling over, she swung at the creature that had her by her legs, catching him across the nose. Blood spurted from both nostrils and, again, his grip loosened. Rolling over, she scrambled on all fours toward the pistol again and managed to grab it just as her assailant landed on top of her hard enough he forced the air from her lungs.

As abruptly as he'd landed on her, however, he sprang upright. When he did, Tessa leveled the pistol at him and fired, putting two holes in his belly. He screamed, clutching his belly and fell face forward, landing on her legs.

Seeing there was another one right behind him, Tessa fired again.

Nothing happened.

She stared up at the creature in stark terror.

He was gasping for breath and glaring at her with fury in his dark eyes.

"I came to help you, woman," he growled in a deep

voice that sent shivers down her spine.

The accent was strange to her ears and the words difficult to understand, but she did understand him. Tessa felt her jaw go slack in surprise. She was still gaping at him when he snatched the pistol from her hand and threw it.

"You ... you speak English?"

He scowled at her. Reaching down, he grabbed her arm and hauled her to her feet. "I speak Saitren," he growled, "Come--before the wreckers come back."

Chapter Four

Tessa felt absolutely no desire to go anywhere with him. She'd seen him fighting with the others. It was possible he was telling the truth and he really had come to help her, but she saw no reason to take it on faith that his motives were purely altruistic. For all she knew he had been one of the gang that attacked her and had simply decided to turn on them for some reason, or they'd turned on him. Moreover, she'd been through hell with others of his species already and she didn't think she was going to be able to feel warmth toward any of them, especially considering his fierce appearance and demeanor. Dimly, she realized her distrust was partly rooted in a healthy dose of superstition--something she'd never considered was part of her makeup, but she couldn't shake it no matter how illogical and unreasonable she knew it to be.

On the other hand, she felt no desire to remain where she was, certainly not if there was a chance any of the others he'd called wreckers might be coming back.

"I came to find the scientists who came here a few days ago. I'm not going anywhere until I check the other lander. I have to know if they're all dead or if there's some chance of finding them alive somewhere."

He caught her around the waist, jerking her tightly against his body, then scooped her legs out from under her. Before she could do much more than gasp in outrage, a strange crackle and a rush of wind filled her ears and they became airborne. Her stomach did a free fall as they rose upward. The moment she looked down and saw the ground falling away beneath her, she ceased trying to break his grip on her, threw her arms around his neck and tightened them in a death grip, burrowing her face against the crook of his neck.

The shock of the attack began to wear off as the warmth of his body seeped into her. Slowly, her senses began to function and awareness crept into her consciousness.

The scent of his skin seemed oddly reassuring and calming. Logically, it shouldn't have. Man had evolved over thousands of years, grown intellectually, achieved far more than early man would ever have dreamed possible, and yet, man was still a mammal, still controlled by certain animal instincts beneath the surface veneer of civilization he had worked so hard to cultivate.

Regardless, this creature was not only not of her own race, he was not of her own species. It would've been natural to distrust and feel repelled or antagonistic toward the scent of a creature not her kind … and on a conscious level, she felt both. On a chemical level, her body was responding contrary to the way it should have. She found it both curious and disturbing, but she could no more fight it as it filtered through her system than she could have fought an injection of drugs into her blood stream.

Her reaction was, pure and simple, a chemical attraction to the male she'd glued herself to like a leach.

That acceptance, however misplaced, lifted her

awareness another level as she moved past a consciousness of warmth only and began to sense the texture of his bare skin as it rubbed against her own with each movement, and the ripple of hardened muscle flexing and undulating against her own softer flesh.

She arrived, at last, at the realization that she was physically attracted to him.

She rejected the notion at once. She was repelled by his likeness to paintings she'd seen of the Christian religion's concept of the devil--and a distant, but unmistakable, thread of personal superstition. It was completely incomprehensible to be attracted and repelled at the same time and by the same physical form.

As an educated woman and a scientist, she knew he was not a supernatural creature. He was very likely much like man, neither all good, nor all evil, but somewhere between the two--possibly leaning more in one direction than the other--but still not an inherently evil creature only because primitive man had perceived him that way.

Nevertheless, her experience with his kind thus far should not have engendered trust, let alone physical attraction.

Unless, her mind supplied, it was empathy and gratitude manifesting itself in a physical response?

Satisfied with that answer, she opened her eyes and shifted enough to look around to see if she could tell where he was taking her. Her heart seized as she saw the tops of the tall buildings she'd flown past earlier. His arms tightened around her as he felt the jolt that went through her.

When she nerved herself to open one eye a sliver once more, she saw that they were headed toward a building slightly higher than those surrounding it. Several balconies jutted out from the top floor. He landed on the balustrade of the largest and then dropped lightly to the tiled floor. The jar of impact jogged Tessa's brain into sluggish function and she focused on willing her reluctant arms to release their hold. As she finally loosened them, he moved his hands to the sides of her waist and she began to slide down his body.

The stone was still uncomfortably warm to the touch, reminding her that the creatures had succeeded in ripping her clothing from her--merely to steal them? Or because they had had rape on their mind?--before this one had freed her. She peered up at his face in the darkness but could perceive only a vague impression of what he looked like. "I'm sorry. I was so upset I didn't even thank you for helping me. What is your name?"

His palms still rode the outward curve of her hips. "Lucien."

His voice made her heart stutter. She couldn't recall ever before having such a reaction only to the sound of someone's voice, but then she couldn't think of anyone she'd ever known with such a deep, resonant voice that it seemed almost to reach inside of her and strum along her nerve endings. "I'm Tessa Bergin--Doctor Tessa Bergin," she added more formally, trying to put some distance between them.

He slipped an arm around her, planting his palm in the middle of her back and urged her toward the door that opened out onto the balcony.

"We came from Earth ... to try to form an alliance and share knowledge."

It wasn't strictly true, of course. The plain fact was that they'd come looking for a handout, willing enough to pay for what they wanted if they had to, but hoping to coax information out of these people for the sake of friendship and good relations.

His lips tightened. "Outworlders have swarmed here like buzzards over a rotting corpse since *the coming*, hoping to pick us clean. I don't particularly condone what the wreckers do, but then neither do I condemn them."

He didn't seem terribly friendly after all, she thought uncomfortably. "The wreckers? You said that before."

"They watch for the ships of scavengers. When they come, the gang brings them down and picks them clean of anything useful--instead of being robbed themselves."

Tessa felt a wave of nausea. No wonder they were so hostile. They'd already suffered a devastating blow and now had to fight to keep what little remained to them. "We didn't come for that! We traveled years to get here. When we left Earth this world was thriving-- we thought we were coming to meet another race of beings. Instead, we saw when we were awakened from sleep that something had happened."

His brows rose. He stopped and turned to look down at her. "And still you came. To offer aid?"

She could tell from his tone even if not for his derisive expression that he wouldn't believe her if she lied. "To study the ... civilization that died here."

His lips tightened, but after a moment he nodded and moved away from her, unbuckling the belt that crisscrossed his chest and secured the scabbard for the blade he carried on his back between his shoulder blades. Grasping the hilt of the sword, he unsheathed it and tossed the scabbard onto a table. Tessa's heart leapt into her throat, but before she could consider that it was highly unlikely that he would've gone to the trouble to bring her here if he'd only intended to kill her, he picked up a wad of cloth scraps, a container, and moved to a padded lounge. Settling on it, he set the container on the floor, took one of the pieces of cloth and began to wipe the blood from the blade.

Tessa watched in revulsion for several moments before she noticed he had a dozen slashes on his chest and arms and legs. The majority had closed already and begun to clot, but several were deeper and continued to bleed sluggishly.

"You're hurt!"

He halted what he was doing and lifted his head. One of his dark brows lifted fractionally higher. "You are observant," he said dryly. "I'll live." He jerked his chin toward a narrow door in one wall. "You can bathe there."

Tessa looked down at herself in dismay. She had blood all over her, but she couldn't tell if it was hers or his--it was all red. Revolted, she moved quickly to the door that he'd indicated and opened it.

There was no artificial light and very little natural light filtered through the small window in the outer wall. "It's dark," she said, her voice tinged with surprise.

He made a sound laced with wry humor. "No power … I had a generator, but I've run out of fuel. There are candescents on that table."

Glancing in the direction he'd indicated, she saw a row of pale stick-like objects and picked one up, looking it over. It did not spring to life and she could see nothing to make it produce light. "How does it work?"

Dropping the sword onto the lounge, he rose and joined her, reaching for another object on the table. When he flicked it, it produced a tiny flame of fire, which he held to one end of the stick. The stick caught fire, producing a flickering sliver of light. Taking one of the rounded disks of metal from the table, he speared the candescent on the spike that protruded from the center of it and handed it to her.

Balancing it carefully, Tessa moved to the door once more and held the light high, peering around. It was a bathroom--or had been. She glanced back at him. "Everything works?" she asked doubtfully.

He jerked his head upward. "There's a cistern on the roof to collect aqua--it works."

Aqua? It was Latin for water.

After studying him curiously a moment, she moved into the small bath and closed the door. He'd said he spoke Saitren--not English. The certainty that his race had visited Earth in the distant past settled inside her and refused to be banished.

They looked too similar to the paintings in the ancient biblical texts for it to be no more than coincidence. The language was not just the same, but it was certainly close enough that she had little difficulty understanding him, or vice versa.

The people of this world had either learned the language of Earth--or humans had learned the language of the Saitren. The languages had evolved divergently, but still close enough to be recognizable as having the same roots. She didn't believe in that kind of coincidence, not when one considered the distance involved.

Setting the candescent down on the counter that surrounded a basin, she studied the waste chamber for several moments and finally made use of it to empty her bladder. A cubicle jutted from one wall and she stepped inside it. It took a few minutes to figure out how to turn it on, but finally she did and was hit by a tepid stream of water. It had obviously been warmed by the sun's heat but was still chilly to her heated skin. Shivering, she bathed herself quickly and turned the water off once more.

It wasn't until she stepped out that she realized she had nothing to dry off with. She'd been too focused on removing the blood to consider what she'd do afterwards. A search of the cabinet beneath the basin produced a small wedge of cloth. It smelled clean so she used it to soak up as much of the water as she could, then laid it over the edge of the counter to dry.

She was still damp when she emerged, and shivering, but she felt better--less unclean in her mind. Some of the blood was her own from scrapes and scratches, mostly from being dragged around naked on the hard ground. She ached and hurt from being slammed around that she'd scarcely noticed the scratches and deep gouges, but none were serious enough to warrant concern. Most of the blood was probably his-- Lucien's, although she dimly recalled that she'd clawed and bit her attackers and thought some of it might have been from that source.

She saw when she emerged that Lucien had lit

several more of the candescents and set them about the large room. A soft, yellow glow broke the shadows here and there, but the room was still far too dim now that the sun had set for her to really tell much about it except that it was a surprisingly spacious room and seemed to be comfortably furnished. The pieces she could see fairly well showed signs of wear and tear, but were not so worn as to appear shabby or rickety.

She saw that Lucien had returned to the lounge and was spreading some sort of oil over the sword. He lifted his head as she emerged, however, and stood up. She moved aside as he headed for the room she'd just vacated.

Hearing the water, she moved toward the balcony. She discovered very quickly, however, that the evening breeze against her damp skin wasn't the least bit comfortable and moved inside once more, finally settling on the edge of a cushioned chair and crossing her arms and legs to try to hide some of her nakedness as she glanced around uneasily.

When she heard the water go off, she stood up. "I suppose it's too much to hope you might have some sort of clothing I could wear?"

He appeared in the door opening, propping his hands against the top of the frame as he studied her. "I had no woman, and thus no reason to have clothing a female might wear."

Had no woman? She was still trying to figure out if there was any significance to that comment when he pushed away from the door frame and started toward her.

She stared at him, grappling with a strange sort of blankness while she tried to figure out what was different about him. She realized what it was as he stepped fully into the light from one of the candescents.

He wasn't wearing his loincloth.

Her heart slammed into her ribcage as her gaze was drawn inexorably toward the pendulum swing of his genitals.

Granted, she had seen very few cocks of the human male variety, but it took no more than a glance to see that Lucien's cock bore only a similarity to those she'd seen. For one thing, it was longer and thicker than any male member she'd seen previously, but the tip was more wedge shaped, and, even in the dim light, she could see some sort of rounded nubs along its length-- almost like nipples.

There was also a small extrusion just above his cock that she'd never seen on a human male.

She didn't know where it came from or even why, because she'd never had a great deal of interest in mysticism, or ancient religion, and she wasn't even certain how she'd remembered the pictures she must have seen of beings that looked very similar to the Saitren--but it popped into her mind as if she was completely familiar with the Christian myth about their anti-god--the devil had a forked tail.

Obviously, humans had had a little more than just a passing familiarity with this race.

Chapter Five

Her survival instincts had atrophied from disuse and determined efforts at civilizing the inner beast of the human. Fear did not penetrate Tessa's shock until she felt his fingers wrapping around her upper arms, preventing escape.

She swallowed, staring up at him while she tried to jog her mind into functioning.

She'd lost any chance of escape long since. He'd brought her to the top of a building at least forty stories tall. Even if she could break free and find a way down other than taking a flying leap from the balcony, he would have plenty of time to catch her before she could escape the building.

If she resisted, he might kill her. At the very least, he would probably hurt her.

Logic told her that she would be far better off to allow him to do whatever he wished and watch for an opportunity to escape ... and still she stiffened, her inner self instinctually cringing as much at the very alienness of him as the suggestion that intercourse was not a choice for her.

As he lowered his head, surprise touched her briefly before his lips brushed almost caressingly against hers.

She'd expected only a brutal assault, not an attempt at seduction, not a semblance of tenderness. A rush of adrenaline flooded her system as his lips skated across hers and then molded to the sensitive surfaces. His breath mingled with her own as he exhaled in a rush, as if he'd been holding it. His taste, like his scent had before, sent a wave of calm acceptance through her, taming the fear inspired adrenaline flow, altering it subtly at first to budding desire.

When he settled his mouth firmly over hers and plunged his tongue inside her mouth, desire burgeoned with far less subtlety, flooding her with the dizzying mind drug of pleasure. The strength seemed to vacate her body so that she quaked with the effort to hold herself upright.

His tongue was rougher than she'd expected-- pleasurably so, making her belly quiver, making the walls of her sex weep in warm anticipation.

She was only vaguely aware of being lifted and carried, feeling a coolness beneath her back. When he released her lips and drew back, she lifted her eyelids with an effort to look at him.

His dark eyes gleamed with both satisfaction and desire as he stared down at her, exploring her with his gaze. The urge to hide herself from his perusal swept through her, but she discovered she couldn't move.

A spark of panic went through her at that realization-- an awareness that it was not merely endorphins pumping through her system, but something far more powerful, something far more debilitating.

He frowned when he saw the touch of panic in her gaze. Catching her wrists, he leaned down, pinning her arms to the lounge on either side of her head as he covered her mouth with his own once more, ravishing her mouth with the possessiveness of his tongue, building the heat inside her and banishing all vestiges of resistance.

She lost track of everything except his taste and the feel of his mouth and tongue as he caressed the excruciatingly sensitive inner surfaces of her mouth.

When he withdrew, he sat back, studying her for several moments and finally caught her legs, pushing them wide until she felt the moist nether lips part and cool air caressed the more perceptive tender flesh. With his fingers, he pushed the nether lips wider, examining her curiously with his gaze before he pushed a finger inside of her.

She gasped at the intrusion but she could not escape it, could neither pull away nor close her legs. She was as bound by what he'd done to her as if she were mesmerized, or he had restrained her physically.

The strange malaise went no further than that, however. Her body responded to the stroke of his finger with sizzling heat and welcoming lubrication.

She glanced down at him when he withdrew his finger at last and a new wave of panic surged through her. His cock had engorged and seemed impossibly huge. The nubs she'd noticed before, obviously erectile tissue, had engorged, as well. He used his hand to part her nether lips wider as he aligned the head of his cock with the opening of her body and began pushing slowly inside, coating his cock with her body's lubrication and using it to ease his passage, pushing inside her no more than an inch or two at the time and then pulling back again until he had coated his cock with her creamy juices.

She'd tensed when he first entered her, anticipating pain, from his size and the nubs that ran along his cock. For several moments as she felt him stretching her, felt her body's resistance to his intrusion she'd

wondered if he could claim her without causing her
harm, but as her body adjusted to his girth and she felt
the stroke of the nubs along her passage, intense
pleasure vibrated through her.

He stopped when he had possessed her fully, driven
so deeply inside of her she was gasping to catch her
breath. Leaning forward, he kissed her with the same,
slow possessiveness of before and as before, weakness,
pleasure and dizziness flooded her, dissipating all
thought of resistance.

When he pulled away once more, he stroked the
blond curls of her mound, pulled the flesh back and
rubbed the tip of his finger experimentally over her
clit. A sharp stab of pleasing sensation went through
her and she groaned. He looked up at her face at the
sound that escaped her. His eyes narrowed in
satisfaction and he transferred his gaze from her face
to her sex.

Drawn by the intensity of his concentration, Tessa
looked down, as well. She saw then that the nub above
his cock had elongated. He guided it toward her clit
where it attached itself in gentle suction that sent
another shock wave of enervating sensation through
her.

Slipping his hands beneath her buttocks, he began to
move slowly in and out of her then, each thrust and
retreat unhurried, stroking the sensitive walls of her
sex in a way that tore the air from her lungs, rivaling
the seductive massage of her clit for dominance in
stimulation. Pleasure jolted through her from her clit
and from the inner walls of her sex at once, converging
to create a sizzling torment in her body.

Within moments, she was moaning incessantly, felt

her body tensing toward release. She squeezed her eyes closed as she reached the peak, hovering unbearably on the edge.

He thrust deeply inside of her and leaned forward to kiss her once more. The stroke of his tongue seemed to temper the tension, allowing her body to cool fractionally, to retreat from the edge of release. When he rose up and began moving inside of her again, her body climbed once more within moments to linger torturously on the edge of release. Minutes passed, hours--she lost all concept of time. Her body was on fire for release and could not reach it. Her entire being seemed to focus on the pleasure he drew from her with each stroke of his cock, with each sucking pull against her clit. Pleasure began to skate the fine edge of pain. Desperation filled her. Her moans of pleasure took on the fine edge of screams, and still he brought her to the peak again and again, only to draw her back once more so that he could take her to the edge again.

She began to beg mindlessly for release, knowing he could give it to her, knowing she was going to die if he didn't.

When she managed to pry her eyelids open to look at him, she saw his flesh gleamed with a fine sheen of sweat, saw his face was contorted with his iron grip on his own need to find release, that his body quivered with the strain of holding back, drawing the pleasure out until it began to skate the edge of torture.

As if sensing her gaze, he opened his own eyes, hesitated. A heavy shudder ran through him. He clenched his teeth, squeezed his eyes tightly, and then let out a hoarse cry of pleasure as his release seized him, tearing his control from his grasp. He began to thrust rapidly then, pounding into her hard, pushing her beyond the precipice she'd lingered on so long that she screamed when her own pleasure burst inside of her blindingly, dragging her mind into a pit of blackness.

When she became aware of her surroundings once more, she felt the caress of his lips moving over her throat and along her cheek, and the stroke of his hand over her body in the appreciative touch of a lover. She lay perfectly still, both soothed and warmed by the gentleness that seemed a perfect counterpoint to the heights of almost unbearable pleasure she'd experienced and the echoes of it that still throbbed through her body. Despite the lethargy that gripped her, however, she felt that her body had been released from whatever it was that had held her, as if her climax had overwhelmed the drug in her system.

Dimly, as she began to float upward toward awareness, she realized it had been some sort of drug-- a natural drug, produced by his body, but still a drug. "What did you do to me?" she asked hoarsely, a thread of accusation in her voice.

He lifted his head, studied her assessingly. "I gave you pleasure," he said coolly, disentangling himself from her and rising.

Shivering the moment his warmth left her, Tessa sat up, pulling her legs up and wrapping her arms around them. He seemed genuinely puzzled by her reaction, but Tessa couldn't tell whether it was because he was surprised that the endorphins had had no lasting effect upon her, or if it was something his body naturally produced and he was surprised at being accused at all.

His phallus was genetically enhanced. She should

have realized that at once, though she didn't know of any human male who'd gone to such lengths in designing the ultimate sex toy for themselves and their lovers, complete with the nubs that had given her so much pleasure her body continued to quake at the memory, and very likely him, as well, since the extrusions were almost certainly as extremely sensitive as any other erectile tissue.

The wonder was that he could endure the pleasure himself without coming almost at once, but she had to suppose that the drug he produced worked upon him in much the same way it had her--allowing her to feel exquisitely but inhibiting her ability to find release.

It didn't occur to her until he'd left the room that it was natural to him, at least in the sense that it was unlikely that he'd had the genetic enhancement done himself. He was almost certainly too young to have been old enough before the fall of his civilization to have had it done.

In any case, she recalled then that she'd thought of the mythology regarding 'the devil' when she'd seen his cock and she realized that his people almost certainly had to have had the ability to manipulate genetics long, long before man had. Where else would the mythology have arisen from?

Whatever it was that their body produced during arousal not only enhanced and prolonged the pleasure, but it made the woman helpless against them--possessed--and unable to exert her own will.

Her resentment faded. He was guilty of nothing more than seduction, which she'd succumbed to. He could not have deliberately made her helpless to resist him when it was surely not something he could control.

A shiver that was part pleasure and part uneasiness went through her. Her body still throbbed with remembered pleasure and showed no signs of returning to its pre-arousal state any time soon.

It didn't take a lot of imagination to realize that it would be all too easy to become enslaved by the pleasure he could produce in her so effortlessly.

Chapter Six

Shaking her thoughts off, Tessa climbed off of the lounge and began to search the dim room for anything she could use to cover herself. She found a length of fabric, at last, but it was far too small to cover as much of her as she wanted. She contented herself with tying it around her waist. Her hair, if she left it down, was long enough to cover her breasts … or at least mostly cover them so that she didn't feel quite so exposed and vulnerable.

When Lucien came out of the bathroom, he was wearing his loincloth once more. His gaze immediately searched the room for her. When he saw her, he seemed to relax. "You have hunger?"

Without waiting for a reply, he moved to what looked like a makeshift kitchen that had been set up in what had once been a bar. Or perhaps the room had been a sort of luxury suite in the days before and had already been set up to prepare small meals? Tessa followed him, climbing onto a stool across the counter from him to watch, although she didn't offer to help.

She supposed it shouldn't have bothered her that he went about his business as if nothing had happened when she'd just had the most unsettling experience of her life, but she couldn't help but be miffed that he seemed to take it in stride. In point of fact, the sexual release had gone a long way toward soothing the trauma of her experience prior to it, something she'd needed desperately to regain her equilibrium, but she still resented the fact that he'd taken advantage of her vulnerability, and she was spoiling for a fight. "Was that why you 'rescued' me?"

He glanced her. "You were in danger. You would prefer that I had not interfered?"

Her lips tightened. If it wasn't just like a man to boil the whole situation down to its most basic element and throw logic in her face. He knew damn well she wasn't objecting to being helped. "I might have negotiated a different price."

His gaze flickered over her face. "You had something else to offer?" he asked coolly.

There it was again, and it irritated the hell out of her that he was right. It was really low to point out that she hadn't had anything else to barter with--and the fact that only a complete idiot would expect the service she'd received to be completely free. She was not only a stranger to him, she wasn't even of his race. It would take some fairly strong motivation to induce someone to take on a dozen or so maniacs with swords and if she'd been in any condition to think straight she would've known what was coming.

Actually, maybe on a subconscious level she *had*.

She hadn't just been jittery from the attack. At least a part of her nervousness from the moment they'd arrived had been from her awareness of him sexually and an unacknowledged sense of anticipation. People were rarely physically attracted without communicating that fact in some way to the person they were attracted to … so it had either originated with her, or him, or it had been mutual from the start, but on some level she had been aware of it.

She liked to think that she would've been willing to risk her life to help someone in need without putting a price on it, but when it came right down to it, would she? With that sort of odds? Maybe. But, in all honesty, probably not.

And she certainly hadn't had any other 'coin' to offer in return for his help.

He glanced down at what he was doing. "I was weary unto death of my own company. You were in need." He looked up at her once more, his gaze moving over her face and down to her breasts. "I offer my strength for your protection and to provide for your needs and comfort. You will give me the comfort of your flesh."

Despite the best will in the world to be insulted and outraged, she felt heated warmth spread over her at his demand.

That didn't change the fact that he hadn't asked and she hadn't--exactly--offered, but then she hadn't objected either. She'd still been perfectly capable of rational judgment when she'd made the conscious decision to give him what he wanted to protect herself--and, as badly as she hated to admit it even to herself, as hard as she had tried to keep from thinking about the situation she'd gotten herself in to, the truth was, she *was* in need of protection.

She was stranded here and she had to face it and accept it. Even if Sinclair was willing to wait, he would leave when she didn't return as she'd said she would. He wouldn't come looking for her.

Silently acknowledging defeat in the unbeatable argument, trying *not* to think about the unthinkable, she focused her thoughts in another direction. "I came looking for a friend--Dr. Layla Lehman. She and the others were supposed to have returned days ago. She would've been in that other lander."

Something flickered in his eyes as he lifted his head and studied her. Sympathy? "The less I know about the wreckers, the more comfortable I am. I saw your ship when you passed by. I was curious enough to go to watch, but if I had not heard your screams, I would not have interfered at all. They are … the most brutal of all the gangs, but they would not have harmed a female, even one such as yourself--not Saitren. Not many survived at all--and fewer females because they were not as strong."

Hope surged through Tessa. "You think she might still be alive?"

He frowned, looking away. "They would not have deliberately harmed her."

"Please! We have to find her, to make sure she's safe."

He set a plate down in front of her that contained something unrecognizable which nevertheless smelled surprisingly appetizing. "I have a female. I do not need another."

Tessa gaped at him in outrage. She didn't know what made her angrier, his assumption that she was now 'his' or his assumption that Layla would also be his if they found her. "And I've no choice?"

He gave her a steady look, his expression hard and unyielding. "Not on this world. Make no mistake. The strongest male will take you. I slew five of my own kind to have you. I will not yield you to another."

Tessa felt a stab of anxiety at his calm assertion that she was a prize up for grabs if anyone stronger or more capable than Lucien came along, but she had absolutely no doubt that he spoke the truth.

Theory when one was safely aboard a ship miles above a world simply didn't compare to actuality. *This* was the reality of her warning about the break down of civilized society. In one stroke, she'd been reduced from an individual of some importance, to a mere female, valuable only because of what she could provide. She should count herself as fortunate that she'd been captured by a male who seemed surprisingly laid back for somebody that had hacked his way through a gang of vicious wreckers to have her. He wasn't exactly talkative. He wasn't warm and friendly, but he had not offered her any harm. In fact, he'd been amazingly gentle with her when he could easily have hurt her only through careless pursuit of his own pleasure. His cock was massive, more than 'weapon' enough to have ripped her internally if he hadn't been so gentle and patient.

"Tomorrow, I will see what I can learn about your friend."

Tessa glanced at him with a mixture of surprise and hope. "You will?"

"I can not promise, but I will try."

Tessa smiled at him in gratitude. Reaching for his hand, she squeezed it. "Thank you."

He looked down at her hand and then met her gaze.

Uncomfortable, Tessa withdrew her hand and they ate in silence for some moments, Tessa with some reservations. The food tasted good, however, even though the flavor was strange to her.

She found herself wondering about the people of this world, and Lucien in particular. "What was it like here … before?"

She could sense Lucien's withdrawal even before she looked at him.

"The past is dead. There is little point in dwelling on it."

It was painful and he didn't want to talk about it. She couldn't blame him. It had been insensitive even to ask. "I'm sorry. I was only thinking that this is a beautiful city."

He frowned, but he relaxed fractionally. "It was."

"You said you'd had a generator for power before. Have you been here, in this apartment, long?"

He glanced around. "Almost a year ... I think. It's not good to stay in one place long unless it's secure."

Tessa looked at him in surprise. "It seems secure here."

A faint smile curled his lips, but it held little humor. "You do not fly."

She felt strangely self-conscious at that remark. Naturally enough, she had been focused upon why he seemed strange to her. She hadn't considered that she must seem as strange to him with her pale hair and skin, with her inability to fly. "I seem ... unappealing to you?"

That time his smile reached his eyes. He glanced significantly toward the lounge. "I seemed displeased?"

Tessa felt a hard blush color her cheeks, but she realized she didn't want to pin him down to anything specific. Whatever he said, he would have had to have felt nearly as strong a shock as she had when she'd first seen the others of his kind. They were just too radically different for him not to have. The wonder was that he'd found her appealing at all, but then she had to suppose just being a female was probably enough. It was hardly flattering, but she didn't know why it bothered her to think that he might think she was ugly or unappealing.

Almost as disconcerting was the realization that she could be far more different than the females of his race even than her outward appearance. Until he'd mentioned the sex, she hadn't considered that the females might also have been genetically enhanced in some way. She certainly wasn't, but then she couldn't imagine what she might do to enhance her desirability through genetics.

When she looked up once more, she saw that he was looking at her curiously.

"You change color. What is this?"

"Embarrassment," Tessa said irritably.

"It is the pale skin?"

Tessa shrugged. "I suppose."

He frowned thoughtfully. "I read of a pale skinned wingless race long ago. Truthfully, I couldn't imagine such a thing existing in reality. I thought it was only tales made up to entertain."

Tessa's heart skipped a beat with a sudden surge of excitement. She was on the verge of telling him her theory when it occurred to her that he would not only probably not find it as interesting as she did, he would most likely be offended.

He shook his head finally. "It has been too long. I do not recall what the story I read was about." He winced when he stood up, holding his shoulder and rotating it.

She didn't doubt that he was sore all over, but she resisted the urge to offer to massage his aching muscles. It was absurd, of course, when she had made no attempt to dissuade him from intimacy, had already lain beneath him screaming at the intensity of the ecstasy he had wrung from her body, but she was reluctant to initiate anything that would give him the impression that she welcomed intimacy. Acceptance, as far as she was concerned, was enough, given the situation.

Instead, she moved around the counter and helped him to clean up.

He surprised her when they'd finished, pulling her close and wrapping his arms around her. She was still trying to decide whether to respond by embracing him in return when he pulled away. Throwing an arm over her shoulders, he picked up a candescent and guided her toward a room beyond one darkened corner that she hadn't noticed earlier.

It was a bedroom, and she immediately tensed, stopping in the doorway. "I should put out the other candescents."

He glanced back, flicking one wing in much the same way one might wave an arm. The gust of air that one motion created extinguished all the candescents at once.

A sense of unreality descended over Tessa. She'd been joking when she'd suggested to Layleh that the beings on this world could look like anything. In the back of her mind, she hadn't truly expected them to look so radically different from themselves.

In a sense, she supposed he didn't. If she discounted the wings, the horns, the skin pigmentation, and the pointed ears, he wasn't that different--one nose, two eyes, one mouth, etc., etc. She had yet to get more than a vague impression of what he actually looked like.

Besides the shock of having to fight for her life that had limited her perceptions, it had been dusk when he'd rescued her. There was very little light in the apartment, but she knew from what she could see that he was as much like her own race as he was different.

She supposed the sense of strangeness came more from the radical change in her circumstances--from Dr. Tessa Bergin to 'the captive mate' in a matter of hours--than anything else. Very likely, she was still suffering from shock, as well.

She felt an odd mixture of anticipation and reluctance as she climbed into bed and lay down. Her body was already vibrating with burgeoning desire merely from remembering what he'd done before, but there was a sense of dread, as well, and the certainty that it could not be a good thing for her to become so addicted to his touch that she craved it--and she was afraid she would if she didn't already

When she felt the skate of his hand over her breasts and down along her body, she turned to meet his gaze, wondering if she could force him to take her quickly, and if that would make him less devastating to her senses.

If she gave pleasure but didn't take it, then he could have no complaints, and she reasoned that she wouldn't have to worry that she might become attached to him in a way that could lead to the sort of pain she wasn't prepared to experience.

She caught his hand and raised up, pushing him to his back. He resisted at first, frowning, but when she followed him down, tracing a path of kisses along his neck and chest, he collapsed back against the bed, his breath rushing from his chest.

She wasn't prepared for the heady rush of desire that consumed her as she tasted him on her lips and tongue. She forgot all about rushing him to take his pleasure, forgot everything except her own pleasure in feeling the brush of her skin against his as she dragged her breasts across his chest, the strength and contour of his muscles beneath her palms.

He jerked all over when she caught his engorged cock in her hand, his fingers tangling in her hair. She ignored it, ignored the harsh cry that escaped him as she covered him with her mouth and sucked hungrily. His hands tightened painfully in her hair, but she was beyond caring. The taste of his cock sent her into a mindless frenzy of need. She licked and sucked at him greedily until he shoved her back onto the bed, grasped her thighs and parted them, driving his cock into her in a frenzy that matched her own. She came the moment he plundered her depths, crying out at the intensity of it and clawing mindlessly at his arms.

He caught her hands, manacling her wrists to the bed as he drove into her in desperate, jerky lunges that quickly brought him to his own release. Shuddering, he sprawled weakly on top of her, breathing raggedly.

Many minutes passed before the haze of bliss began to lift. A sense of both irritation and wry amusement touched Tessa as she drifted downward from the ecstatic haze of repletion and surfaced into awareness again. She had certainly driven him to take her quickly, but it had not gone off just the way she'd envisioned it.

She looked up at him almost warily when he finally managed to lever himself off of her. He studied her for several moments and then rolled away, righting the two of them on the bed and tucking her against his side.

"That was ... quick," he said neutrally.

Tessa bit her lip. "I suppose from that remark you didn't particularly care for the Earth custom."

A shudder went through him. He swallowed audibly. "I could have pleasured you longer...," he said finally.

Thoroughly relaxed, feeling surprisingly safe, Tessa stifled a yawn. "You pleasured me thoroughly," she murmured.

Some of the tension left him. Tessa hadn't realized until that moment that he was tense.

She sighed, feeling a stirring of despair. It would've made her life a lot easier if he was as brutally wicked as he appeared.

She discovered when she woke that he *had* made it easier. He was gone, but he'd left her a little reminder that he still considered her a captive--and that he did not trust her any more than she trusted him.

He'd placed a collar and chain on her.

Chapter Seven

Tessa decided she must have been unconscious instead of merely sleeping, but then, considering the day she'd had she supposed that would've been a fairly accurate assumption.

She was so stiff and sore from fighting for her life the day before that she could barely move. When she finally managed to sit up, she still hadn't managed to pry her eyelids up, but the sound that greeted that movement and the drop of cold metal against her body brought her wide awake.

She stared at the chain uncomprehendingly for several moments before she picked it up and followed the links of metal to the uncomfortable tightness around her throat, which proved to be a collar.

Leaping from the bed, she followed the chain from the bedroom, pacing to the length of it. She had just enough to reach the bathroom and pretty much everything inside the apartment. She could not get any closer to the balcony, however, than six feet from the windows.

She was so furious that it took her a little while to realize the significance of that limited reach.

Lucien said the strongest male would take her. He wasn't taking any chances that she might get near enough to the windows to be spotted and possibly coveted.

After calling him every foul name she could lay her

tongue to, she began to search the apartment for anything she could use to remove the collar. She'd searched every inch of the place twice before she finally gave up. There was nothing resembling a knife or scissors, nothing that she might use to pick the lock on the collar.

Eventually, her anger burned itself down to a slow simmer and she went into the kitchen to find something to eat. He used fire for cooking in some sort of brazier. She stared at it for several moments, but the chain could certainly not be burned and she wasn't about to stick anything hot enough to burn through the leather anywhere near her throat.

The food he had was processed and packaged, which meant that it was at least ten years old. Undoubtedly, it was still good, though, or she would've been feeling it today.

Naturally, nothing was recognizable, beyond the fact that she could tell which things were meat type substances and which vegetable. Her stomach, weak after such a long period of abstinence, rebelled at the unfamiliarity of the food, but she managed to eat a little.

There was no sort of refrigeration, naturally, since there was no energy source beyond fire. She drank more of the tepid water that traveled by way of gravity into the apartment from the cistern on the roof.

When she'd finished, she sat staring at the walls for a while and finally decided to set the place to rights since she'd turned it upside down looking for a way to free herself. She had nothing better to do, nothing else to do at all beyond staring at the walls and sulking.

Considering the circumstances, the apartment was

surprisingly comfortable. Everything seemed to have faded, but she could see that it had originally been decorated in cool colors, pale greens and blues, shades of purple and lavender. The windows were nothing but embrasures, covered now with thin, pale drapery. An almost constant flow of air streamed through them, keeping the temperature relatively comfortable.

She stared at the drapery speculatively for a while, envisioning swathing herself in one of them. She stood as close as she could to it for a while, waiting for a gust of air strong enough to bring the fabric within reach, but finally gave up.

She doubted it would make a great deal of difference anyway. If Lucien wanted to have sex with her, he would do so, regardless. In any event, it occurred to her that familiarity bred contempt. Eventually, her nakedness would cease to provoke his lust, she was sure, and he would expend his lust and lose interest. When he did, he would cease to guard her so closely and she would find the opportunity to escape.

She had no idea of where she would escape to. Her lander was a pile of debris now. The other one too, as far as she'd been able to tell, and if the wreckers had stripped it as Lucien said, then it certainly was, whether it had been too damaged by the crash to use or not.

They were capable of space travel, however. Somewhere on this world there must be a useable ship.

Realistically speaking, even if she could get loose from Lucien, she doubted she would have time to find a working ship and rendezvous with the *Meadowlark* before Sinclair high tailed it back to Earth. She would've liked to have made the attempt--she was trying very hard not to allow hysteria to creep in at the thought of being abandoned on this brutal world--but it seemed unlikely she would even get the chance to try if Lucien meant to chain her whenever he wasn't around to watch her.

It was better, she thought, to focus on a future escape and the possibility of locating a ship that would carry her back to Earth than to allow despair or hysteria to gain ground. Otherwise, she would be incapable of doing anything to help herself. If she couldn't locate a ship ... she'd face that when the time came. At the very least, she might have the chance to free herself from being the sex slave of an alien being that unnerved the hell out her.

As the day wore on, boredom chased away the dregs of anger that had remained as well as her anxieties.

Fear was her first reaction when she heard the meaty thud of a body landing on the balcony. She was still trying to decide whether to try to hide or to go see if it was Lucien when he filled the doorway, bracing an arm on either side.

Tessa stared at him curiously, her heart still tripping over itself with a mixture of fear and relief. It was several moments before she noticed the blood streaming from his side and down his thigh. After a moment, as if he'd only stood in the doorway long enough to gather his strength, he pushed himself away from the frame with an effort and moved toward her unsteadily. She was too paralyzed to move, merely gaping at him as he wove a drunken path to her where she sat on the lounge and finally dropped to his knees in front of her.

Grasping her collar, he pulled her to him, fumbling

with something. She felt the collar loosen and fall away and drew back to look at him. He sat back on his heels, wavered for a moment and finally collapsed back against the floor.

It was enough to penetrate the shock that had held her rooted to the spot. She scrambled off the lounge and bent over him.

"Thought I would not make it back to free you," he said in a voice slurred with weakness and pain.

Tessa swallowed, subduing the horror that thought evoked, of being left chained to die when she ran out of food and water. Apparently, that had been uppermost in his mind, as well.

She looked down at the wound in his side. "What happened? My God! You're bleeding all over the place."

"Did not want to tell me," he mumbled without opening his eyes.

"Who? Who didn't want to tell you what?"

"Where she was."

Tessa stared at him blankly as a different kind of horror set in. "You got this trying to find out about Layleh for me? Oh God, Lucien! Why didn't you tell me it was so risky? What can I do? I don't know what to do!"

She saw, finally, that he was beyond telling her.

She had to stop the bleeding. He'd bled so much already he would die from blood loss if she didn't stop it. Refusing to consider that he might already have lost too much, she jumped up and looked around frantically before rushing over to the nearest window and tearing the drapery down. She tripped over it in her haste to get back to him, landing on her knees painfully.

Ignoring the pain shooting up through her thighs, she formed a wad with the cloth and pressed it to the wound.

He gasped, jerking, then wrapped his fingers around her wrist with surprising strength. She slapped his hand away. "I've got to stop the bleeding."

It wasn't stopping though. It soaked through the wad of fabric so quickly it scared the hell out of her.

Leaping to her feet, she ran frantically around the apartment, looking for something to hold the wound closed. She'd taken the place apart looking for something to pick the lock or cut the collar, but she'd been focused on that. She couldn't remember anything that had looked like medical supplies--no laser of any description to burn it closed--no sewing supplies. She'd searched the apartment from top to bottom before she thought about the drapes. Rushing to the rod, she stared at the hooks that had been used to hold the fabric in place and finally leapt up, grabbing the rod and snatching it down.

Her stomach cringed at the thought of piercing his skin with such thick, dull spikes, but he was going to die if she didn't do something to close the wound.

She refused to consider he might die anyway, that there was probably a better than even chance that the sword that had pierced his side had ruptured a vital organ.

Landing on her knees beside him again with a pile of the clips, she mopped as much of the sticky blood from her hands as she could and pinched the wound closed at one end with shaking fingers. "This is going to hurt like hell," she warned him, bracing herself and stabbing it into him before she had time to reconsider.

He let out a hoarse cry, his shoulders coming up off the floor. The sound of his pain tore through her like a knife. Mopping tears from her eyes, she grabbed another clip, pinched the wound together and stabbed the metal into his flesh. This time, she heard his teeth grinding, saw his body flinch, but he managed to keep from crying out. By the time she'd managed to dig four clips into him, she saw that the bleeding had slowed.

Lucien seemed to have passed out.

She was glad. It was traumatic enough just having to do it. Seeing the pain she was inflicting was tying her stomach in knots.

She dug the last two clips into him and collapsed back on her heels, shaking, trying to fight off the blackness that was threatening to overwhelm her. Finally, she dragged herself up and staggered to the basin, splashing water on her face until some of the weakness subsided. When she thought she could make it back without fainting, she filled a mug with water and went back to him. Dipping a clean section of the fabric into the mug, she cleaned as much of the blood away as she could.

God only knew what was happening inside of him, but the blood wasn't pouring out any more.

She didn't realize she was blubbering like a baby as she ripped the drapes into strips to bandage Lucien with until she felt his hand on her knee. When she looked down at him, all she could see was a shifting blur. Mopping the tears from her eyes, she saw that he'd regained consciousness.

"An Anjel took her."

Tessa sniffed, fighting the urge to burst into tears

again. "She'd dead?"

He frowned, obviously confused. "Do not know. Enemies of the Saitren, always were. He stole her from the wreckers and took her to Henven--across the sea."

Tessa stared at him blankly. "You're talking about another being from this world?"

He nodded. "The Anjels."

She shook her head as if it would help to sake the bizarre sense of unreality. "We'll talk about that later-- when you're better. Do you have anything to kill germs? I washed the wound, but I should put something on it to keep it from getting infected."

He frowned, apparently unfamiliar with the terminology, but finally nodded and sent her to a cabinet in the bedroom. She found the medical kit she'd been too frantic to find earlier, but, except for the bottle of antiseptic, there wasn't anything in it that would've done any good anyway, only a few bandages. Returning with the container, she poured antiseptic liberally over the wound. He flinched, hissing in pain, but said nothing.

Forming a pad with a length of the drape, she placed it over the clips and then began to wind strip after strip around him. When she'd tied it in place, she got up and went to find something to carry more water, it having occurred to her that he would probably have other wounds. He was too bloody for her to tell as it was.

She found a dozen more wounds that looked new, but they didn't seem to be too deep. Dousing them with the antiseptic, she bandaged the worst and finally moved away from him, propping her back against the lounge while she rested, trying to calm her shaky nerves, trying to think if there was anything else she might do for him.

The truth was, she hardly even knew basic first aid. She'd never had to tend anything worse than a hangnail. She felt weak, nauseated, weepy.

She shook it off when she saw he was trying to struggle up. Bending over him, she placed her palms on his shoulders. "You're liable to start bleeding again. Just lie here for a while. I'll try to help you to the bed later."

When he complained of thirst, she moved to the kitchen for water and returned. Lifting his shoulders, she held the mug for him until he'd drunk his fill and then set it aside, settling his head in her lap and staring down at his face.

It was the first time she'd had the leisure and the light to actually study his face. With a touch of surprise, she saw that he was a strikingly handsome man. His black brows were straight, winging upward on the outer edges toward his hair line. His eyes were surrounded by a thick veil of long, dark lashes, his nose straight and well formed, his square jaw and chin strong, his lips sensual without being either soft or the least bit feminine.

He looked young. She wondered if he was even as old as she was or if it was merely that his dark skin aged better than fair skin. He'd adapted well enough to the change in his world to seem to indicate that he had still been fairly young when the disaster had overtaken his world, but then it seemed unlikely that he could have survived at all if he'd been very young.

She stroked his hair from his cheek, noticing for the first time that his black hair was streaked, in an almost striped pattern, with locks of deep red hair. Except for the long black hair on his head, and his brows, his body was otherwise hairless. She hadn't thought about it until that moment, but he hadn't even had hair in the pubic region.

When she dragged her gaze back to his face, she saw that he'd opened his eyes to study her. The irises of his eyes were almost as black as the pupils, but a thin, deep red circle surrounded the outer edge.

She blushed at being caught studying him. "I'll get you something soft to prop your head on."

He looked like he might object, but finally he merely closed his eyes again.

He began to shiver when night fell. Tessa checked his bandages but saw little leakage since she'd closed the wound. Rousing him, she helped him into the bedroom and onto the bed.

His skin was warmer than her own even when he wasn't ill, but even so, he felt hotter than normal. Retrieving more water, she bathed him until he felt cooler and then spread the coverlet over him.

He got worse as the night wore on. Tessa tried not to think about the wound, tried not to think about what she was going to do if he died and left her alone. Instead, she concentrated on doing what she could to keep the fever down and keep him comfortable, dragging a chair over to the side of the bed when she became too weary to stay awake any longer and dozing in it for short respites.

Toward morning, he began to thrash about on the bed, muttering. She bathed his heated skin again and finally climbed into bed beside him. He quieted when she pulled his head against her breasts and stroked his hair soothingly.

When she woke again light was filtering into the room. She felt as if she had a firebrand burning a hole through her chest. Easing out from under Lucien, she fetched more water and began bathing him again, changing the water when it got too hot to do him any good. Her shoulders were aching from lugging water from the bath to the bedroom by the time she had cooled him down enough she thought it was safe to take a break.

She'd just emptied the water from the bowl she'd been using to carry it in when she heard a noise outside that made her heart jerk in her chest.

Stopping, she lifted her head to listen, but the sound was unmistakable. Dropping the bowl, she rushed to the door of the balcony and outside. In the distance, she could see the *Meadowlark* descending from the clouds. Her heart began pounding in her ears so hard it drowned the whine of the engines. She stared at the silvery sliver as it passed, heading for the landing area, her body tensing for action, shivering with the need to race from the apartment and try to chase it down.

She couldn't, of course. Lucien had sealed the door leading up to the apartment from the building and she certainly couldn't fly. Even if she could've gotten from the apartment to the street, there was no way to reach the site in time.

Even as she stared at the vanishing shape, however, feeling desolation steal over her, she saw a swarm of black dots descend upon the ship. In horror, she watched as the wreckers attached themselves to it.

Abruptly, the ship did a ninety degree ascent and disappeared into the clouds once more.

She told herself she was fiercely glad they'd

managed to save themselves, but it took an effort to swallow against the knot of misery in her throat.

They were gone. They'd come for her, but she'd missed them and she was never going to get home again.

When she finally turned toward the door to the apartment once more, she saw that Lucien had dragged himself from the bed. He was braced in the door frame, his dark skin bleached of color.

Chapter Eight

Swallowing her despair with an effort, Tessa surged toward Lucien, wrapping her arms around his waist before he collapsed. "You shouldn't have gotten up. I'm not sure I could bear it if I had to redo those clips."

He dropped his arm to her shoulder, leaning against her as she struggled to guide him back toward the bedroom. He looked even paler than before by the time he collapsed onto the bed. Tessa shifted him around until he was fully on the bed and pulled his shoulders up to shove a pillow behind his head.

His skin felt cold and clammy now.

She bit her lip, wondering if that meant something worse than the fever. Finally, she settled on the side of the bed and began to work the bandage loose. When she got down to the pad, she saw that blood had adhered it to the wound.

"Just rip it off," he said through gritted teeth.

She slapped his hand when he reached for it. "Leave it alone, damn it! Play macho some other time. I don't want it to bleed again."

Retrieving the antiseptic, she soaked the bandage with it.

He let out a hiss of pain, but she ignored him.

"Your people came for you."

She looked up at him, trying to fight the wobble in her chin. She knew the moment she opened her mouth she'd start squalling, however, and instead of trying to answer merely looked away again. She wasn't going to think about the fact that she was stranded here. She just wasn't. She didn't think she could bear dwelling on it.

Scrubbing the tears from her cheeks with the heel of her hand, she lifted one edge of the pad carefully. Seeing the liquid had softened the dried blood, she jerked it off. A few bright red dots of blood oozed from his skin, but otherwise the wound seemed to have sealed itself. Blood beneath the skin had formed a bruise that covered an appalling area, but she couldn't see any sign of bloating that might indicate he was still bleeding inside.

Maybe he'd been lucky enough after all that the man who'd stabbed him had managed to catch nothing but flesh?

The fever descended on him again, but it didn't seem as bad as before. Toward evening, he struggled from the bed and wove a path to the bathroom. When he came out again, he was soaked, shivering, his hair dripping water. Tessa sought patience. "You shouldn't be taking a shower until that wound has closed better."

Ignoring her, he made his way back to the bed and fell into it face first, then groaned at the pain that shot through him.

Sighing, Tessa dried him off the best she could and rolled him over to check the wound. He'd discarded the bandage. The wound looked angry, but his skin was so red already that she wasn't certain even of that. Finally, she doused it again with antiseptic--just to be on the safe side.

He caught her wrist. "If I did not know better, I might begin to think you do that simply because you enjoy inflicting pain."

Tessa narrowed her eyes at him. "You're absolutely right! I get my jollies every time I pour it on you!"

He released her, but the moment she'd set the container down, he grasped her and dragged her across his chest. She stared down at him with a mixture of surprise and dismay. He'd hardly managed to drag himself back to bed. It hadn't occurred to her that he might still have enough strength to retaliate if she provoked him.

"You could have left me to die."

It honestly hadn't even occurred to her. "You nailed the only door out of here shut," she countered. "I can't fly, remember?"

"You could not pry it open? Is that why you stayed?"

Her lips tightened. "I didn't try."

"Why?"

It was a simple enough question, but the answer was too complicated for her to sort through it, especially when she couldn't help but be aware of her bare breasts pressed tightly against his chest, of his scent, assaulting her nerve endings, stimulating currents of desire. She swallowed with an effort. "I don't know. You were hurt. I didn't want you to die ... especially because of me."

His gaze flickered over her face, as if he could discern the truth. Finally, he released his grip on her wrists and speared his fingers through her hair, pulling her down and melding his lips against hers. Dizziness swept through her with the first hot rake of his tongue along her own. She fought the urge to yield, the desire to return his caress. "You shouldn't. You can't do this--not now. You'll reopen the wound."

For several moments, she thought he would ignore her plea for reason. Finally, he released her.

She scrambled off of him and off of the bed.

"Tomorrow, we must leave this place and find another."

"But ... you need to recover. You need rest."

"You may have been seen. I can not take the chance when I can not defend you. It will be risky enough even to stay the night."

"You could barely make it across he apartment and back without passing out," Tessa pointed out.

"I will manage. It would be preferable to go, I think, than to stay and be skewered again because I can barely lift a sword to defend myself."

That seemed inarguable--and very unnerving. Leaving him, Tessa gathered up his sword and looked around for anything else she thought might make a handy bludgeon. When she failed to find anything, she smashed a table and pulled the legs off of it. Returning to the bedroom, she piled the weapons inside and went to the kitchen for food and water.

Lucien, she noticed, was watching her with a mixture of curiosity and amusement. Irritation surfaced. Ignoring him, she checked to make sure she had everything she could think of that they might possibly need for the evening and then moved into the bedroom and started piling everything she could move in front of the door.

"What are you doing?"

"If you keep smirking at me I'm going to pick up one of these table legs and beat you over the head with it-- what does it look like I'm doing?"

"Barricading us in?" he hazarded.

She turned and gave him a narrow eyed glance. "I suppose you have a better idea?"

"I suppose you considered that we have no avenue of escape?"

Tessa took a deep, sustaining breath and quelled the urge to say something sarcastic. "You said someone might have seen me. How are we supposed to defend that room out there when it's wide open to the outdoors?"

He shrugged. "We?"

"If one of those thing--men come in here, I'm sure as hell not going to crawl under the bed and wait for them to drag me out."

Something flickered in his eyes. "Things?"

Tessa blushed. She stared at him wide eyed, then looked away, trying to think of some word she could substitute that wouldn't sound as offensive. Unfortunately, nothing came to mind. She'd laid that ugly thing out between them and now she couldn't figure out how to remove it. "I figured we could block the door and at least they couldn't catch us off guard."

"The things?"

Shame filled her. She had every reason to hate them besides the ingrained racial prejudice of generations of Earth people who'd thought of the Saitren as evil incarnate. She didn't think, or feel, that way about Lucien, but why would he believe her? "Do you think, maybe, you could cut me a little slack here? I'm trying to cope with this the best I can."

She turned to look at him but saw he had rolled onto his side. She swallowed against a hard knot of misery. "I'm scared, OK? I didn't mean it the way it sounded."

When he didn't respond, she gave up. Anger replaced

her remorse. Stalking to the barricade she'd just finished erecting, she began shoving everything out of the way. When she'd cleared the door, she grabbed one of the table legs and stalked across the apartment to the exit and began hammering on it.

"What are you doing?"

She glanced at him, saw that he was standing in the doorway of the bedroom and went back to beating on the door. "I'm leaving, damn it! The way I see it, we're even. You saved my life. I saved yours. If you're well enough to get pissy, then you ought to do just fine."

He caught the bludgeon on her next swing, jerking it out of her hands. She whirled on him angrily, but he'd obviously anticipated a furious retaliation. He blocked her swing, then jerked her tightly up against him. Catching her hair in one hand, he tugged until her neck arched and her head was tipped back so that she was forced to look at him. Fury gleamed in his eyes. "I prefer honest hate to deception acquiescence," he growled, lowering his mouth to hers and kissing her bruisingly. She struggled, but he only increased the pressure until he'd forced her lips to part. The moment they did, his tongue penetrated the broken barrier, laying siege to her senses. She struggled to hold on to her anger, but she wasn't nearly as angry with him as she was with herself. More powerful even than the drugging effect of his kiss, the remorse she'd felt flooded back.

She ceased to struggle, caressed his tongue with her own before the weakness swamped her.

She was only vaguely aware of being lifted and carried back into the bedroom, of the cool softness of the sheets beneath her back. She saw, though, when he caught her wrists and pinned them to the bed that he was angry still. He'd misinterpreted her attempt to apologize as an attempt to deceive him with her submission. Obviously, he had realized from the first that she had submitted before only because she knew she had no choice, not because she was grateful for his help, not because she felt like she owed him a debt she should repay in whatever coin he demanded--but because she was trying to deceive him into letting his guard down.

She could not evade the heated desire he infused in her with just his kiss, however, could do nothing but submit because he'd stolen her will.

She didn't even realize he'd released the bruising grip on her wrists until he pushed her thighs apart and she felt the pressure of his cock as he merged his flesh with hers. She gasped, squeezing her eyes closed as she felt his slow but insistent possession, felt her body yield reluctantly to the immensity of his distended flesh, clenching around him and impeding his progress even as her sex flooded with moisture that helped him to claim her.

It took an effort even to open her eyes. When she managed to lift her eyelids, she saw that he was staring down at her, his face taut with repressed need, his eyes glittering. His desire fed her own, lifting her higher on the pyre of carnal pleasure. Panting, she focused on the need to feel him claim her completely and tilted her hips to meet his next thrust so that he sank deeply and she could feel his flesh fully imbedded within her. It sent a surge of warmth and gladness through her that went beyond the thrill of being possessed completely,

of feeling their bodies merge. A moan escaped her as
the nodules along the length and breadth of his cock
massaged the exquisitely sensitive surfaces of her
passage, sending sharp arcs of white hot sensation
along her nerve endings to her pleasure centers.

He closed his eyes, breathing harshly. His hands
shook faintly as he skated them caressingly along her
body, cupping her breasts. She arched her back, lifting
to meet him.

She heard him swallow, watching as he leaned closer,
as his face filled her gaze. For several moments he
hesitated, his breath teasing her lips, his lips hovering
so close to hers that she could feel the heat of him.
Finally, he tipped his head, kissed the corner of her
mouth and brushed his lips along her cheek. Dipping
his head, he sucked a tiny fold of flesh along her throat
between his lips, and all the while he moved his hips in
a languid undulation that stroked his cock slowly along
her passage and back again, sending fresh waves of
almost unbearable stimulation along her nerves until
they were jerking with tension, sizzling with the need
to find release.

She lifted one hand and gripped his shoulder as he
moved lower, digging her fingers into his flesh,
arching upward as his lips grazed the upper slope of
her breasts. He lifted his head, studying her face as he
reached between them and parted her labia, guiding his
secondary appendage so that it fastened onto her clit,
pulling at it in gentle suction that sent a jolt of ecstasy
through her as he moved his cock along her passage in
concert.

She cried out, gripped him tighter as she felt her body
escalating toward release.

He covered her mouth with his own then, kissing her deeply, entwining his tongue with hers. Despair filled her as she felt release elude her, felt her body trapped by his so that she could only writhe feverishly with need beneath him.

Instead of building her to the breaking point as he had before with slow, tortuously wonderful strokes, when he broke the kiss, he lifted away from her and braced his palms on her knees, spreading her thighs wide for his access and began to pump his cock into her in short, hard thrusts that tore cries of agonizing pleasure from her, that consumed her with heat and pushed her rapidly toward her peak once more.

She groaned when he leaned down to kiss her once more, certain she could not bear the pleasure any longer. "Lucien," she whispered against his lips.

He stilled, gasping harshly. Lifting his head slightly, he gazed into her eyes for a long moment and then buried his face against her neck, driving deeply into her in forceful, rapid strokes that sent her screaming into mindless oblivion.

A vague awareness drifted through her mind as she felt him scoop her into his arms, felt the warmth of his body as he molded her against his length, the stroke of his hands along her back, the brush of his lips on her face. The dreamlike quality of it barely penetrated the warm cocoon of repletion that enveloped her, however, and like a dream, it drifted easily from her consciousness.

It was barely light when the sound of quiet movements nearby penetrated Tessa's subconscious and jerked her into fearful alertness.

Chapter Nine

Lucien flicked a glance in her direction when Tessa started awake and sat up, looking around nervously. Realizing that it was Lucien who'd awakened her, she fell back against the bed, closing her eyes and trying to fight the urge to roll over and go back to sleep. Finally, it penetrated her tired brain that Lucien had said they needed to move to another location today, that it was no longer safe to stay where they were.

Rolling from the bed, she headed toward the bathroom on unsteady feet.

Feeling only slightly more alert when she emerged, she glanced around the living area, wondering if she should take anything … not that anything belonged to her. She spied the remains of the drape she'd used to bandage Lucien, however, and moved toward it. Tearing off a couple of strips, she tied her hair up with one and wrapped the other around her breasts. It was hardly a fashion statement, but it was too hot to wrap more fabric around herself and she felt too exposed with nothing at all.

Lucien, she saw when she turned, was watching her.

Without a word, he turned toward the exit. Setting the bundles down that he'd gathered, he drove a thin length of metal through the space between the door and jam and pried it open.

Tessa followed him, picking up the bundles. Although she wondered why they would be taking the stairs instead of flying, she wasn't going to question him about it. In the first place, she didn't particularly care for sailing through the air forty stories up when the only thing between her and certain death was Lucien's grip on her. In the second--there didn't seem to be much sense in reminding him of her aversion to flying things with horns that looked like demons. She could tell just from looking at him that he was still spoiling for a fight.

She was sorry. She'd tried to tell him she was, but as badly as she felt, she also felt that her reaction was understandable and entirely justified and that he should have taken that into consideration. She'd been victimized and terrorized by the first of his kind that she'd ever seen. She would have to be a complete moron *not* to hate and distrust them. Maybe she had been predisposed to, but, except for Lucien, none that she'd met so far had done anything that made her feel that she was being unfairly judgmental.

Moreover, no matter how well he treated her, Lucien had made it clear that she was his captive, that he considered *her* a 'thing' that was now his. If anyone was being unreasonable, he was.

The only reason she still felt guilty about it, and felt he had any justification in being angry about it, was because, however unintentional, it had been a 'below the belt' kind of blow and she knew it. It was one thing to insult somebody about something they did or said on purpose, another thing entirely to insult them about something they couldn't help or change.

She stopped worrying it over in her mind after a while. It wasn't something that could be undone or fixed. He'd get over it. It wasn't as if he didn't think of her as a 'wingless' thing. It wasn't as if she cared anything about him beyond the fact that he was, currently, her lifeline, or that he cared anything at all about her beyond the fact that she was useful as a warm body to thrust his cock into whenever the mood struck him.

The passion between them was just that--a violent chemical/animal attraction that was more intense than anything she'd ever experienced in her life and almost more than she could endure. If she hadn't had a strong heart, she'd have been dead by now from the heart palpitations he gave her every time he took her to the very heights of pleasure and then held her there endlessly until her climax was so explosive she lost consciousness.

It was almost as scary as it was addictive, but whatever doubts she'd entertained that he wasn't well aware of the effect he had on her had been banished. He *expected* his kiss to leave her helpless to him. If anything, she sensed that he was, perhaps, a little surprised because it must not effect her in quite the same way as it did Saitren females--which certainly stood to reason since she wasn't one.

She had a feeling that the discovery wasn't exactly a welcome one to him. She hated to admit it, even to herself, but it bothered her to realize that he probably found her lacking in some way.

It took them hours to make their way down the twisting stair that led to the ground floor. She was too preoccupied with her thoughts to notice much to begin with. By the time she emerged from her self-absorption, she was already beginning to feel the effects of too little sleep and too much unaccustomed exercise to care much about looking around. It finally penetrated the fog of her chaotic mind, however, that the dozen or so misshapen bundles of rags they passed in their descent, weren't bundles of rags. They were the decaying remains of a devastated race of people.

She felt ill when she realized it. She wondered what had happened, but Lucien had already been very clear on the fact that he didn't consider it a subject for discussion. She supposed she understood. Everyone dealt with grief in their own way and she didn't suppose avoiding it was any more unhealthy than wailing over it endlessly. In the end, one way or another, there was nothing anyone could do except put it behind them and go on and whatever helped them to cope and go on faster was probably for the best.

She didn't think he could've been old enough at the time to have had a wife, or mate--whatever they considered them on his world--but she supposed that all depended on how early in life they mated, how old he actually was and how long it had been. She couldn't rule out the possibility that he'd lost a family of his own as well as parents, siblings, aunts, uncles, cousins--friends.

She'd always considered herself unfortunate for not having close connections, but maybe she was actually fortunate, protected from the pain of separation because she had no one to lose. She missed Layla and they had only been friends.

They stopped when they reached the ground floor, rested, and ate a little of the food that Lucien had brought. She had only to glance at Lucien to see that he was still weak and in a good deal of pain. He was sweating profusely, despite the fact that even she, who wasn't accustomed to the temperature, was only mildly uncomfortable. His coloring was pale and pasty and his hands shook.

She was pretty sure it didn't help at all that he'd fucked her half the night, but she'd tried to dissuade him from exerting himself. She couldn't argue with the fact that he knew far more about the dangers of his world than she did, but it seemed to her that his weakness was a danger in itself and that they'd be better off to hole up a few days in one of the other apartments in the building than to risk being caught in the open while he was still so weak.

"But what do I know?" she muttered under her breath, not even bothering to address him. "I'm just an empty headed female, right? And captives don't have any rights anyway."

He slid a narrow eyed glance her way but otherwise gave no indication that he'd heard, or understood, anything she'd said.

Standing abruptly, he packed their supplies up and grasped her arm, hauling her to her feet and pushing her ahead of him. "I don't know why I'm leading when I haven't got a clue of where we're going," she muttered after a few moments.

"Because I don't trust you to follow."

"Well, then it's a damned shame you didn't think to bring the leash!" she snapped furiously..

He pulled her to a stop, set the pack he was carrying down and dragged the damned thing out. Tessa was too shocked even to think about protesting until he'd already grabbed her around the throat. By then it was too late. When he'd fastened the collar around her throat, he looped the chain around one arm, allowing her just enough to trail along behind him.

She glared daggers at his back as he tugged her to the front of the building and finally stopped once more at the doors, leaning out to study the street, the surrounding buildings and the sky. Finally, he turned to look at her. "Unless you want to be captured and taken off to service a dozen or more 'things' I would advise you to keep quiet and stay close."

A shiver of fear skated down her spine. Wide eyed, she turned to survey the area around the building, as well.

Despite the fear, irritation surfaced as he tugged her outside--as *if* she could do anything *except* say close when he had a damned leash around her neck!

She didn't comment. In the first place, she had no desire to be caught by a dozen or more of those 'things' and used by all of them. In the second, she wouldn't have put it past Lucien, in his current mood, to choke her with the collar if she did say anything.

She glared at his back resentfully, however, as they moved slowly down the sidewalk, hugging the walls of the building and stopping every few minutes to scan the area for any sign of threat.

It seemed to her that they would've been better off to have waited until dark. Surely that would've increased their odds?

Or were the Saitren nocturnal in their habits?

Lucien didn't seem to be, but she couldn't say for certain that he wasn't. Maybe he went out during the day because he knew the others usually slept then?

Instead of traveling straight down the thoroughfare the building fronted on, they wove a crooked path along narrow alleys. They seemed to be traveling in a northerly direction, which would take them closer to the heart of the city.

After a few hours, Lucien led her inside another building, checked it out, and finally settled to rest. As tired as she was, Tessa looked around with interest. The area where they'd stopped looked as if it must have been a store of some kind. It had been pretty thoroughly looted and trashed, but there were shelves and tables that looked as if they'd been designed to display wares of some sort.

The looting seemed to indicate that there'd still been a fairly large number of living when the social structure had begun to break down--this sort of wild, mindless theft generally only occurred when people still thought they could profit from the things they stole. Once it was borne in upon them that they needed things to survive, not luxuries that wouldn't actually do them any good, they tended to be far more selective in what they took.

Regardless, whatever had happened on this world had been global, and it had been fast. What, she wondered, would fit that scenario? More importantly, was the planet really in recovery? Or was there still a threat?

She couldn't completely dismiss it, but she'd already been here almost a week and she couldn't tell that she felt any different physically. In any case, they'd already ruled out the likelihood of any sort of biological warfare.

She'd begun to think they had been less than accurate in their assumptions about the race, or races, of this world, however. There was absolutely no doubt that they were intellectually advanced, but, assuming her theory was correct and they actually had visited Earth in the distant past, and so terrorized primitive man that they still retained a racial memory of their fear of the Saitren, then they had a very long history of being both advanced and brutally aggressive. The breakdown of their societal structure had almost certainly accentuated their natural tendency toward aggression, but it seemed to her that they'd 'adapted' far too quickly to their more primal selves to ever have had much more than a thin veneer of civilization to begin with.

What she'd seen of the remains of their civilization also seemed to indicate a preoccupation with more 'earthy' interests. The architecture was beautiful and lavish, but from what she had seen so far, more dedicated to the pursuit of pleasure than the pursuit of knowledge.

There were no overt signs of a fascination with technology. True, there'd been plenty of time to demolish much of what there'd been, but there should have been debris from all sorts of things, at the very least. They carried swords. There weren't any manufacturers of modern weapons left, but there should still have been plenty of usable weapons laying about--unless they'd used up everything on each other right after the downfall.

Theirs was a truly alien culture in every respect. Humans had been trying to breed the violence out of themselves for generations, but she couldn't see that the Saitren had made much effort in that direction at all.

She wondered if their enemies, the Anjels, were very different from the Saitren. It seemed likely that there would be at least as many similarities between the two races as there were between Earth's races, but she had a strong feeling that the Anjels he referred to were part of the same Earth mythology as the Saitren and beyond being winged beings and man-like, they were vastly different from the Saitren.

The thought led her to her friend's plight and she wondered if Layleh was faring any better than she was.

It began to seem unlikely that she would ever know. Lucien would certainly not allow her to persuade him to go searching for Layla among his enemies and she didn't think, even if she managed to get loose from Lucien that she would be able to find Layla on her own. It wasn't like she had directions. It wasn't as if she could ask--and Lucien had said Henven was across the sea.

Late in the afternoon, Lucien chose a building, from what she could see at random, and went in to explore. When he'd apparently assured himself that they had the building to themselves, he secured the chain he'd tethered her to and left without a word.

Tessa was too tired by that time to feel much resentment. The bed she collapsed on smelled musty with age, but it didn't fall apart and she was too tired to care about much else.

Chapter Ten

They rested for a full night before moving on again. Bit by bit, the city yielded to countryside. Occasionally, Tessa spotted a strange animal, but that was rare and she couldn't decide whether or not it meant the animal population had been as devastated as the higher beings, or it if was only because the animals were wild and naturally cautious.

The flora seemed to be thriving. The wooded areas had crept up to the edges of the paved roads they followed. Wildflowers created carpets of multi-colored blossoms beneath the towering trees. An occasional insect buzzed past her.

She never saw any birds. She didn't know why she expected to, but most worlds did have flying creatures.

This one too, but they seemed to be the higher order of animals.

They didn't see any Saitren, not even in the distance. Once they'd left the city behind, Lucien didn't show any indication that he expected to.

They had traveled two days beyond the city before Lucien seemed to find what he'd been searching for, a relatively comfortable and isolated structure that looked as if it had belonged to someone of extreme wealth. The building itself was huge, and surrounded by a thickly wooded park, which was hemmed in by a ten foot tall, spiked wall. It looked like what it was, a luxurious fortress.

Lucien had not touched her since the night they'd left. Tessa wouldn't have admitted it under torture, but she was far more disappointed than she was relieved. She told herself that she was relieved. She tried to make herself believe the lie, but she knew better. On a conscious level, she *was* relieved. Unfortunately, physically, she was already addicted.

When Lucien had settled her, he set about searching the building for the furnishings that were available that remained intact. For days they worked in virtual silence, building a comfortable 'nest'. Contrary to what Tessa had hoped, and expected, he did not release her. The chain was long enough to allow her a good deal of freedom, and privacy when she needed it, but she could not go far.

After several days, when he had scavenged what was available, Lucien began to make short excursions for supplies. Each time he left, he was gone a little longer, which meant he was having to travel further and further a field to find the things he wanted.

When it finally dawned on her that Lucien didn't trust her at all--certainly not enough to allow her enough freedom to escape--and wasn't likely to any time in the near future, Tessa began timing him. She spent the time while he was gone searching for something she could use to pick the lock on the collar. When she finally found several thin metal tools she thought might work, she hid them and waited for the next opportunity.

The moment he left the following day, she grabbed the tools and moved into the bathroom where she could use the mirror to see what she was doing. She was so nervous it took her almost an hour to pick the lock. She wasted no more time once she was free. Quickly gathering several days' worth of food and water, she left the building and struck off through the woods heading east.

She had no desire to return to the city. It was far too dangerous, but she felt relatively safe in the rural area. Once she'd found a place to stay and a food supply, she decided, she would consider what to do next.

Despite her haste, the wall was no more in sight when she heard the unmistakable sound of flapping wings. Instinctively, her head whipped toward the noise and her heart seemed to stand still in her chest. Lucien landed no more than twenty feet from her and it was obvious from the look on his face that he was absolutely furious. Whirling, she threw everything she was carrying down and ran for all she was worth, turning and heading down the barrier wall, which she couldn't hope to surmount with Lucien so close. Despite the lead she'd had and the speed fear had given her, she could hear him behind her, rapidly overtaking her.

He caught her within minutes, grabbing her around the waist and jerking her to a halt. She whirled on him, fighting to free herself, but she'd been no match for his strength when he was weakened from his injury and he was completely recovered from that now. Catching her wrists, he forced her arms behind her back and manacled them together with one hand. He caught her face with his other hand, digging his fingers into her cheeks until she was forced to open her mouth for him and then kissed her until he'd sapped the will to fight from her and she went limp.

Despair filled her as she felt him scoop her into his

arms and launch himself into the air. Within minutes, he'd landed on the deck of the building and strode inside.

She was still too weak and disoriented even to protest when he dropped her crossways the bed and pulled the rags off that she'd used for clothing. With a mixture of consternation and confusion, she watched as he bound one wrist and ankle to the foot of the bed and the other wrist and ankle to the head.

She was not left long to wonder why he'd tied her in such a manner. As the drug from his kiss began to wear off, she realized that he had served her up for himself to use as he pleased. Her hips rode the edge of the bed. Her splayed legs left her sex completely open and vulnerable to whatever he wished to do.

He stood watching her, waiting until he saw full awareness return to her eyes. When it did, he very slowly and deliberately removed his sword and scabbard and set them aside before turning and removing his loincloth.

Tessa swallowed convulsively, fearing the anger in his eyes and at the same time unable to prevent her body from reacting with desire to his.

Leaning over her, he placed a palm on either side of her head, studying her for several moments. "You are mine," he growled.

She twisted her head to the side to avoid his kiss as he bent to claim her. Catching her face, he held her, covering her mouth with his and kissing her deeply, insistently until she felt herself descend into the drugged euphoria that sapped her of will and any awareness beyond her body.

She was wet for him. Her passage yielded to the

insistent pressure of his cock as he exerted his claim, pushing slowly but inexorably inside of her until his cock was fully sheathed within her, impaling her, stretching her until she had to struggle to catch her breath. Pleasure blossomed inside of her as she felt the rake of his nubbed cock in retreat, then press into her again. He watched her face as he stroked her, knew when the drug that held her enthrall began to lose its potency and her body began to climb toward release by the escalating of her cries of pleasure.

Each time it seemed to be within her grasp, he stilled, leaning over her to kiss her once more until she was floating in a heated, haze of want and need that kept her from fulfillment. Time seemed to stand still as she rose over and over almost to the release she began to desperately pray for, only to slide down once more without reaching it.

When she finally reached a state of such agonizing pleasure that she was barely conscious, he withdrew from her altogether.

Moments passed before her body cooled enough for her to realize that the pleasure had been taken from her. Slowly, awareness returned. When she looked around, she saw that Lucien had left her alone.

Shaken, confused, she lay staring up at the ceiling, trying to ignore the throbbing of her body, trying to calm her racing heart. Minutes passed, an hour. Frustration and anger began to set in.

She closed her eyes as the discomfort of being left unfulfilled slowly eased. A shadow fell over her. When she opened her eyes, she discovered that Lucien had leaned over her. She twisted away, but again he pried her jaws apart and raked her tongue along hers, stroking her, filling her with mindless need.

Despite the drug induced submission, she flinched when she felt his cock pressing into her once more. When he'd pushed fully inside of her, he parted her labia and attached his appendage to her clit. A shudder went through her as pleasure jolted through her.

It seemed to her dazed mind that he tortured her endlessly with pleasure, withholding fulfillment each time she came close to reaching it. After the sixth time of taking her almost to climax and then withholding it, she lost count, could no longer focus her mind at all.

She was barely conscious when he withdrew and left her once more.

She moaned in dismay when he came to her again. To her surprise, he untied her, however, allowing her to attend her needs. She tried to bathe, but she could barely stand even to touch herself. When she'd finished, he led her back to the bed.

She struggled, fought him until he subdued her and tied her once more as he had before.

If she'd been able to, she would've wept when he began once more, would've begged for release. Instead, she could do no more than writhe helplessly, trying to fight the scalding tide of desire.

Exhaustion overcame her when he left her the fourth time. She wasn't certain how long she slept, but he woke her after a little while and began the exquisite torture all over again.

Morning light was filtering into the room before he finally left her to rest. Her body was on fire by now, however, and it was a long while before her weariness overcame the throbbing of her body and claimed her.

When she awoke, the sun had already traveled across

the sky and was descending once more. Her body ached all over from the unaccustomed usage as well as the tension that had never found release. She could barely walk when he dragged her from the bed and walked her to the bathroom to attend her needs and shower. When she'd finished, he led her to a table and set food in front of her. She stared at it without a great deal of interest but finally ate.

She'd thought her ordeal was over until she finished and he led her back to the bed. Despite the certainty that it was useless, she struggled anyway. He left her when he'd tied her once more, long enough that full awareness returned, long enough to begin to dread what she knew was coming.

When she saw that he'd come to stand over her again, her heart nearly stopped. She couldn't stand any more. She knew she couldn't. "Don't! Please! I swear I won't try to escape again."

He leaned over her, planting his palms on either side of her head, his expression immovable. "Two days. Next time, four."

Tessa swallowed, licked her lips. "But--I've already learned my lesson." Next time, she'd make damned sure he didn't catch up to her.

Either he saw the lie in her eyes or he'd set out with a certain punishment in mind and he had no intention of stopping until he'd exacted it. He swallowed her protests beneath his tortuous mouth, drowning her in that state of dim awareness where her whole body became focused on its pleasure centers and nothing else.

The vague hope had surfaced while she waited for him to come to her again that he'd fucked her to the point of insensitivity. In point of fact, the opposite was true. The more he did to her, the more sensitive she became. Nor did the chemical he infused in her body with every kiss lose its effect or potency. Instead, it seemed to exert more control over her and leave her with less will, seemed to hold her longer and longer each time at the edge of completion.

She groaned as she felt his fingers along her cleft. Expecting to feel the intrusion of his cock, fire shot through her as she felt the rake of his tongue instead. Her body shuddered, quaked, fought its way upward toward release as he stroked the tender, ultra sensitive flesh with his tongue, sucked her clit, teased it until she was nearly mindless.

When she thought she couldn't bear it any longer, he stopped.

Despair descended over her as she felt the euphoria claim her again, holding her tightly in its grip. She began to think his tongue was more tortuous even than his cock. Again he lavished her endlessly with the stroking caress of his tongue, the suction of his mouth on her clit until she thought she would die of the pleasure.

She'd didn't realize that he'd changed tactics until much later. After tormenting her over and over, bringing her down only to take her to the heights of pleasure once more, he allowed the chemical to wear off and brought her to such an explosive climax that she passed out.

Her body was still quaking from release, long denied, when she became aware of her surroundings once more, became aware that Lucien had come to punish her yet again.

A ray of hope emerged. He'd brought her to climax, rung every ounce of pleasure from her, she was certain, that she had in her.

She found it made no difference. When he trust his cock inside of her and began caressing her passage, her body responded as if it had never found release. He took her to the edge of release over and over before he finally allowed her to have it, allowing himself release, as well.

She saw when he untied her and allowed her to see to her needs that it was dark outside. She'd lost all track of time and wondered vaguely if night had only just fallen, or if it was nearing sunrise of the second day.

Either night had only just fallen, or he had decided to punish her longer. Hours passed in a heated haze of mindless pleasure that culminated each time in a release so powerful she lost consciousness. She was too weak even to stand on her own at first when he released her several hours later.

She'd thought stimulation without any chance of release was the worst he could do to her. She discovered that hours of stimulation followed by explosive release was almost as bad, and far more debilitating.

She didn't even try to rise when he untied her the next time. She was fairly sure she couldn't, nor walk even if she managed to get off the bed.

To her relief, he merely moved her over, lay down beside her and dropped to sleep. More relieved than she would ever have imagined possible, Tessa released her tentative grip on consciousness and sought the true bliss of absolute oblivion.

When she woke at last, the collar was in place once

more and Lucien was no where in sight.

Chapter Eleven

Tessa had no idea of how long she'd slept. It was nearly dark when she awoke, but it had looked much the same outside when Lucien had finally allowed her to sleep. She finally decided, however, that she must have slept throughout the day ... maybe even two days.

Weak and stiff, it took a strenuous effort of will even to maneuver herself to the edge of the bed. She had to make several attempts to stand before she succeeded. Even when she had, she found she couldn't walk without excruciating pain. She finally managed to make it to the bathroom, however.

She did not make it back to the bed. She'd scarcely made it halfway across the room when she fainted. When she came to, she felt Lucien's arms around her as he lifted her and carried her to the bed.

A shiver skated over her as he brushed her hair from her cheek. He hesitated, seemed to study her for a moment and finally turned and left.

When he'd gone, Tessa rolled onto her side, putting her back to the room, feeling faintly ill. With no more than a casual touch, he had summoned the heat inside of her as surely as if he'd stroked her intimately. After two days of being fucked into insensibility, she would've thought she was far more likely to be repelled by his touch forever afterward than attracted, but it seemed that she'd been right to begin with. She'd developed a complete dependency upon him ... become so addicted to the way he made her feel that she craved it even now.

Desperation swamped her. If she stayed much longer she would never be able to free herself from him. She would, in truth, be completely and totally his, body, mind and soul--possessed.

Unfortunately, the trip to the bathroom had convinced her she was in no shape even to think about attempting escape again--not so soon. And by the time she'd recovered enough to consider trying again, very likely he would begin to watch her more closely.

It took her several days to work the soreness from her body. Lucien, when he was around, watched her broodingly as she limped from the bed to the bathroom and back again. It unnerved her, but when he made no attempt to approach her, she began to relax.

He seemed to spend most of his days 'inventing' comfort, or finding supplies, always careful to make certain there was an abundance of everything that they needed.

She pretended to be sleeping when he climbed into bed beside her at night, but he always pulled her against him and she couldn't prevent the quivers that skated through her when his scent filled her nostrils and the heat of his body enveloped her. Eventually, the soothing stroke of his hand along her back would calm her, however, and she slept in truth, but she always awoke feeling tense and unsatisfied, feeling as if she needed him to take her again.

Within two weeks of their arrival, they had running water. Tessa had watched Lucien curiously as he worked outside, running pipes from the well up to the roof. Once he'd begun working on the roof, naturally, she could no longer see what he was doing, but she found out when he came into the apartment and turned on the water. As he'd done before, he had set up a cistern on the roof, except this one was set up so that he could hand pump water from the well whenever there was little rainfall.

Tessa was both impressed and amused. Obviously, necessity was the mother of invention and he was sick of lugging water up to the second floor in buckets. They did not have hot water, unfortunately, because there was no fuel to power a generator, even if they'd had one, but at least the plumbing worked.

Tessa had never been particularly fond of domestic chores, particularly when there were no labor saving devises to help out, but captivity bored her out of her mind. Even scrubbing floors with a rag was better than sitting in one spot and staring out the window all day.

Lucien allowed a week to pass before he approached her for sexual favors again. As glad as Tessa was of the reprieve in one respect, it was wearing on her nerves and it gave her far too much time to dwell on the two nights he'd spent fucking her into idiocy. Watching him toil outside in the sun, the sweat gleaming on his body, the flexing and bunching of his muscles with every movement, made it nearly impossible for her to get her mind on anything else as hard as she tried to throw off the effects of the powerful pheromones he'd released in her.

She knew when he came to stand over the bed and study her speculatively, that he meant to take her. A shiver of anticipation skated over her. He frowned. After a moment, he took her hand and drew her from the bed, removing the clothing she'd fashioned from scraps of cloth. She was shaking by the time he'd undressed her. Weakly, she wilted onto the bed, waiting while he removed his own garment. She caught her breath and held it as he moved over her, torn between desire and anxiety. Pushing her thighs apart, he settled between them, propping his upper body off of her with his arms.

Tessa let out a shaky breath, staring deeply into his eyes, trying to calm her thundering heart beat.

He swallowed, let out a harsh breath. "You are afraid of me now."

Tessa blinked in surprise. If she was afraid of anything, it was herself, her dependency. She didn't think that there had been any point since she'd met him when she'd been afraid of Lucien.

She was on the point of telling him she wasn't when it dawned on her that, as wonderful as he'd made her feel, he had intended to punish her for trying to escape, to teach her that she belonged to him and there *was* no escape. And it had been torturous. She shivered again at the memory.

She wasn't certain, then, what answer he sought.

After a moment, when she said nothing at all, he shifted, placing his palms over her upturned hands, lacing his fingers through hers. She held her lips up for his kiss when he leaned toward her, sighing as she felt his lips moving over hers in a gentle caress, plucking lightly at the sensitive flesh with his lips. Dizziness washed through her as he traced the surfaces with the tip of his tongue. Instead of covering her mouth with his own, he moved along her cheek to her ear, nuzzling it, tracing the whorls with the tip of his tongue.

Heated sensation traveled downward, along her neck and across her breasts, lifting the fine down of her body in search of stimulation.

Releasing her hands, he scooped his arms beneath her shoulders, burying his face against her throat. "Tessa," he whispered, his voice raw with need. "Love me."

A little shock wave of surprise went through her at his words, jolting her out of the warm lethargy that had begun to seep into her pores as she felt his heated flesh against hers, and his scent and taste filled her. After a moment, she lifted her hand to stroke his cheek, then skated her palm along his shoulder and arm. When he raised his head, she tilted hers up to kiss his throat. Slipping both arms around his neck, she lifted her head, rubbing her cheek along his, nuzzling his ear, catching his earlobe between her teeth in a gentle love bite.

He groaned. Rolling onto his side, he speared his fingers through her hair, cupping the base of her skull in his palm as he opened his mouth hungrily over hers and thrust his tongue past the fragile barrier of her lips. Moaning in pleasure, Tessa stroked his tongue with her own, closed her mouth around him and suckled his tongue.

A shudder ran through him. Gasping hoarsely, he broke the kiss and moved along her throat once more, shifting downward, nibbling at her flesh with his lips.

She cried out his name, clutching his head and shivering with delight at the faint abrasion of his tongue when he opened his mouth over one breast and ran his tongue over her distended nipple, circled it and finally sucked it into his mouth. Heat flashed through her, arrowing downward into her belly so that the muscles of her sex spasmed with need. She was shaking with desire by the time he released her nipple and moved to its mate, running her hands restlessly over his back and shoulders, clutching at him.

Skating her hands down his back, she stretched to reach his buttocks, arching her hips against him. He shifted upward at her insistence, nudging her cleft with the head of his cock and she spread her legs wider, arching to meet him.

Slipping one arm beneath her thigh, he supported himself with his other arm, watching her face as he claimed her inch by excruciating inch until he'd buried his cock deeply inside of her. A shudder went through him as her muscles clenched around him, gripping him tightly. For a moment, he seemed to hold his breath, hovering, fighting for control.

When she caught his face between her palms and pulled him down to kiss him, he kissed her with gentle savagery, lifting his hips in a slow outward stroke and then thrusting into her. An urgency seemed to grip him, however, and he broke the kiss, increasing the pace of his strokes swiftly until he'd set a savage rhythm that lifted Tessa to the peak of passion within moments and thrust her over the edge.

She cried out, sucking a love bite on his neck as her body spasmed with pleasure. The throes of her passion seemed to send him spiraling out of control. Tessa tightened her arms around him as she felt him shudder with his own release.

Sated, gasping for breath, Tessa felt as if her body had been completely sapped of energy. She was already half asleep when Lucien rolled off of her and tucked her against his side.

When she woke, the morning sun was filtering into the room. She lay drifting in dreamy contentment for a little while, remembering the night before with pleasure. Within a few moments, something began to tease at her mind, however. It took a little while to realize what it was.

Lucien had kissed her and it had felt wonderful--but unlike all the times before, there had been no lassitude that followed, no sense of drug induced euphoria.

Chapter Twelve

Rising abruptly, Tessa strode to the bathroom and climbed beneath the shower. The chill morning water took her breath for several moments, bringing chill bumps to her flesh. She welcomed the jolt of unpleasant reality. It pushed another unpalatable reality further into the back of her mind.

Unfortunately, the thoughts refused to stay there, crowding back into the forefront of her mind each time she dismissed them. Finally, she dropped into a chair in the living area and covered her face with her hands.

She had comforted herself for weeks with the certainty that she was a victim, that she couldn't help but respond to Lucien because he produced some kind of natural aphrodisiac that took control over her, making her helpless.

She'd told herself that it was something even Lucien couldn't control.

But he'd controlled it the night before.

And she'd responded to him with every bit as much feverish need as if she'd been unable to help herself.

She *had* been unable to help herself.

She'd wanted him for days and when he'd invited her to indulge her desire to make love to him, she'd welcomed the chance to stroke his skin, to taste and caress him with her lips. And it had driven her into a mindless need equal to anything that he'd done before.

How much of what she'd done was self delusion, she

wondered?

Thinking back, she realized that she couldn't recall but one other time when he'd not used his power of control over her, but it didn't particularly comfort her because she'd been wild for him then, too.

"God!" What was wrong with her? He was an alien! He wasn't even human! How could she want him at all, much less with such ... consuming abandon! Especially after the reception she'd gotten from the others of his kind!

And why had Lucien decided, now, to show her that he didn't even need to use the aphrodisiac to have her?

Was that it? To prove to her that she belonged to him?

She shook those thoughts off. She sure as hell couldn't understand him when she couldn't even understand herself.

How had she found herself wrapped up in a web of wanting, needing, belonging, when all she'd ever wanted to do was to find her friend and find a way home?

She supposed, deep down, she had always known that was pure fantasy, that, for good or ill, she'd been abandoned on this world to make what she could of her life. Maybe it was that fear of being completely alone on this alien world that had made her so susceptible to Lucien, but she realized she'd been lying to herself for a very long time, almost from the first, in fact.

From the moment Lucien had told her that he'd grown weary of his own company, it had touched a chord inside of her, opened her to him as surely as if he'd uttered some magic incantation. She hadn't just been upset that she had a wounded, and possibly dying, man on her hands when he'd come back to her hurt. She'd been nearly hysterical because it was Lucien.

It was disturbing to realize that no amount of enlightenment or education could truly remove a person from their basic animal instincts. She hadn't been guided by her head. She'd been drawn to mate with the strongest male. She might just as well have only just crept from a cave.

She wanted to reject it. She simply wasn't prepared to face it at the moment. Rising, she tried to keep her hands busy in the hope that it would also keep her mind occupied, but she found herself wondering if her hope of going home really was an impossible dream.

Much of what the Saitren had built still stood. She hadn't seen a single space craft since she'd arrived, but that didn't mean there weren't any left that were operational.

The problem was, even if it was true, how would she ever find one?

She would have to go back to the city.

She shuddered at that thought, wondering if she actually wanted to go home badly enough to risk meeting up with the wreckers.

She was so busy debating the matter under her breath that it was several moments before she discovered Lucien had returned. She jumped when she turned around and found him watching her curiously, wondering guiltily if she'd been muttering loud enough that he'd overheard her.

He frowned, looked down at the bundle in his hands for several moments and finally offered it to her. She looked at the package in surprise, but finally took it and unwrapped it. Something deep blue and almost silky in texture slithered out of it. She caught it before it hit the floor and held it up to examine it.

There were two pieces--a long skirt that was slit up one side to the hip and a kerchief top that had narrow crisscrossing straps in the back. Abruptly, tears filled her eyes. She swallowed convulsively, trying to blink them away.

He shifted uncomfortably. "I liked this one. It's the color of your eyes. But there were others."

"No!" she finally managed to say. "It's ... it's beautiful."

He lifted a hand to stroke her cheek lightly. "*You* are beautiful."

Tessa bit her lip, fighting the urge to burst into tears. She'd spent the entire day trying to think up some way to leave him and go home. She couldn't think of anyone who'd ever managed to make her feel so wonderful, and so wretched, both at the same time.

Clearing her throat, she moved away from him abruptly, retreating toward the bathroom. "I'll just try it on," she said quickly, slamming the door behind her. Dropping onto the lip of the tub, she covered her mouth with her hand, trying to fight down the urge to cry. He would hear her if she gave in to it and he would wonder why she was carrying on like her heart was broken.

She didn't know why she felt the desperate need to cry herself. Finally, she set the clothing carefully aside, turned the faucet on and began scooping cool water over her face. Slowly, the urge receded. She was far from calm, however. Her hands shook as she discarded the rags she'd been wearing and fastened the skirt around her waist. She had some difficulty twisting the straps behind her back and fastening them to the top, but finally managed it.

Pulling the tie from her hair, she combed it out until it gleamed and took a deep, sustaining breath before she left the bathroom.

Lucien was standing at one of the windows, staring out into the night.

She saw from the stiff set of his shoulders that he realized his gift hadn't gone over as well as he'd expected. She felt bad all over again.

When he turned at last, she smiled at him tentatively.

His gaze raked her from head to toe before it met hers once more.

"Thank you," she said, feeling more than a little awkward.

He nodded, but he was frowning uncertainly. Finally, he moved toward the small kitchen area he'd built along one wall.

"No! I already prepared something," she said quickly. "Sit. I'll get it."

Dinner was awkward. Each time Lucien glanced at her, he seemed to be torn between desire, and a feeling of ill usage. It did nothing to calm Tessa's rattled nerves. Even worse, the domesticity of the situation gave her a bizarre sense of unreality.

She'd never thought of herself in such a situation at all, let alone sitting across from an alien.

She couldn't even figure out why that kept popping into her mind. She hadn't honestly thought of him as alien since she'd met him--not really. When she thought of him at all, she only thought of him as

Lucien, a desirable man.

It was as if she'd suddenly stepped back from herself and was looking upon both herself and Lucien as a stranger might.

She realized finally that she was trying to distance herself from him. She had been all day, ever since she'd realized that she felt more for Lucien than she wanted to.

It was just plain insane to feel anything at all. She was his captive. He didn't even trust her enough to allow her to roam freely.

Because he didn't see in her what she saw in herself.

He believed she still saw him only as an alien who'd captured her and he was afraid if he let her go she would leave.

And maybe she would.

She didn't know anymore, but she hated the confusion. She hated the turmoil of her emotions.

When they'd finished eating, she cleared the table and cleaned up by herself. Lucien settled in a chair in the living area and watched her. When she could delay no longer, she joined him. To her surprise, he pulled her into his lap, settling her against his chest and wrapping his arms around her.

Oddly enough, it hadn't occurred to her before that he was often demonstratively affectionate toward her. Mostly, it had seemed to her that it was after sex, the sort of lover's caress that one got when one was fortunate, but she realized suddenly that that wasn't true at all. Lucien always cuddled her close and stroked her when they went to bed at night, whether they had sex or not. He was just as likely to caress her cheek, or her back, or her arm if she came close enough at any time.

She'd thought the night before when he'd said 'love me', that he'd meant he wanted her to take the initiative and make love to him. Had he meant it that way, though?

"Tell me about your home world," he murmured, smoothing her hair back from her neck and dropping his lips to the patch of flesh he'd uncovered.

Her body reacted instantly, her nipples standing erect and tenting her top.

"What do you want to know?"

He leaned away from her and gathered her hair into his fist, kissing the back of her neck. A shiver skated along her back. "Are they all like you?"

She chuckled shakily. "Like me in what way?"

"Pale skin, pale eyes--hair like sunshine."

"No. Long ago, we were many races. It's not so much that way anymore. We've mixed so much, but each race had their own unique traits and you can still see it in a lot of the people. We are many colors."

"Blue?"

She turned to smile at him. "No blues--except the eyes--white, like me, brown, yellow, red, black-- except, of course, nobody's really any of those colors, just skin tones. I mean, I'm not just white. I've got a little pink, maybe a tiny bit of yellow and even a little brown from the sun."

"Red? Like the Saitren?"

"Not ... not really."

"This is why I seem very different to you?"

"Uh ... yes."

"The wings? No race on your world has wings?"

"No."

He was silent for several moments. "All races on Nadryl have wings."

"Nadryl? That's what you call this world?"

He nodded, releasing his grip on her hair and smoothing it.

"How many races on Nadryl?"

"Two."

Tessa turned to look at him in surprise. "Just two?"

He shrugged. "Once there were others."

She nodded. "But you mixed?"

"No. We killed them."

If it was a joke, it was certainly in poor taste. When she shifted around to look at him, however, she realized that he was perfectly serious. "All of them?" she asked weakly.

"Some fled to other worlds, I think."

"But ... why?"

He shrugged. "They were different--not like the Saitren."

Tessa couldn't think of anything to say for several moments. "The ... Anjels, they're like the Saitren, then?"

He frowned. "No. They are pale like you. I thought you were one of them when I first saw you, but then I saw you had no wings."

It was discomfiting to learn that she looked like the enemy of the Saitren, particularly when it was obvious their hatred for one another ran deep. "So ... why didn't you wipe them out too?"

"We tried. We fought many battles--here and on other worlds, too."

Tessa stiffened. "When?" she asked a little breathlessly.

"Long ago--aeons. We were a war like people then."

Tessa rolled her eyes. "Fortunately, you've mellowed a lot since then," she said dryly, but she couldn't help but be relieved that the awful things he said his people had done had happened long, long ago.

He lifted his dark brows at her tone. "Yes."

Tessa waited to see if he would say more. When he didn't, she prodded him. "So, your people conquered space travel long ago and traveled to many different worlds?"

He hesitated. "Yes."

She frowned. It was like pulling teeth to get anything out of him. "And your people visited a lot worlds?"

"Conquered many worlds. It was one of the things we clashed with the Anjels over. They tried to claim many of the same worlds. After a time, however, we saw that we had spread too thinly through the universe and returned to our home world."

She'd considered mentioning it before and discarded the idea, but she was curious to see what he'd say about it. "Your people came to my world--to Earth, I think. I've seen ancient texts with paintings," she said after a moment.

He'd been stroking her arm almost idly, but at that, he stilled. "That is why you looked at me that way," he said quietly. "I should have known the hate and fear were deeper."

Tessa didn't know how to respond to that--she wasn't even certain of what incident he was referring to, unless he was talking about when they'd first met--but she supposed there really wasn't much she *could* say. "I was fearful because they were trying to kill me," she said finally. It was at least a part of the truth.

He sighed, wrapping an arm tightly around her waist. "Your own people never did evil things?"

"They did a lot of horrible things … long ago." She thought it over. "They still do some pretty terrible things, actually."

"But they hate us, even now?"

"Most people, now, don't even believe you ever existed, but … they would not trust you, no."

His arm tightened around her. "It was always the same … everywhere that I went."

Tessa twisted around to look at him again, frowning. "*You* have been to other worlds?"

He nuzzled her cheek and nibbled at the corner of her mouth. "When I found the cure for the plague. It was too late for us, but they had already begun to move on to the next world. I tracked them for many years, but even on those worlds that were advanced enough to understand, that could have used the cure to save themselves--they hate all Saitren still and did not trust me enough to take what I offered."

Chapter Thirteen

There was no subtle way to ask where the ship was that had taken Lucien to the other worlds he had visited. Tessa wracked her brain trying to think of one and came up empty. She knew if she asked him point blank, he wasn't likely to answer and it would only increase his distrust.

Dismissing it for the moment, she relaxed against him, enjoying the nibbling kisses he traced across her face and lips, and the burgeoning desire they created inside of her. After a moment, she shifted around and placed one hand on his shoulder and her other palm along his cheek, fitting her lips to his. He released a heavy sigh as if he'd been waiting for the offer. Tightening his arms around her, he captured her lips beneath his and traced the seam where they met with his tongue. She parted her lips in invitation.

He slipped one hand upward to palm the back of her head, his fingers tightening in her hair as he responded with heated need to the invitation, plunging his tongue across the sensitive threshold and stroking it across hers. The heady arousal his intimate caress evoked was so potent she thought for many moments that he had released the chemical intoxicant into her system, but the leaching of strength from her was no more than her own body's response to the taste and feel of his flesh as their mouths mated.

Feeling the need for more contact, she shifted again,

straddling his lap and rubbing her cleft against the hard ridge of flesh that pressed against his loincloth.

Grunting, he slipped a hand between them and released his cock from captivity, pressing down on her hips as she moved against him.

Desire heated their bodies. The intoxicating aroma of their combined scents perfumed the air, making their hearts race and their lungs labor. When Lucien broke the kiss at last, he was gasping for breath. Holding his gaze, Tessa unfastened the straps to her top and tossed it away, then reached for the closure on the skirt and discarded that, as well. Arching her back, she brushed her breasts up his chest as she slipped her arms around his neck and began to nibble at the lobe of his ear.

His hands slipped down to ride her hips, tightening as he curled his hips upward, sliding his cock along her cleft. The nubs of his cock teased her delightfully, sending heat spiraling through her belly. After a moment, she pulled away from him. Coming up on her knees, she grasped his cock and aligned the head of it with her nether mouth, pressing down steadily and sheathing him within her body. His hands fell idle on her thighs as he watched her, watched their bodies slowly joining. He rotated his hips, pulling out slightly to spread her body's lubrication more fully along his cock before driving into her more deeply.

Tessa caught her breath, holding it as she felt the wonderful abrasion of the nubs of his cock raking along the sensitive walls of her passage. She dug her fingers into his shoulders, expelling the breath she'd been holding in a rush as she felt him fill her completely, felt her nether lips grinding against his belly. She held the sensation to herself for a moment before she began moving so that his cock stroked her the length of her passage in a shattering caress.

Lucien caught her hips, slowing her pace, lifting his hips upward and thrusting in counter to her movements. "It feels so good inside of you, Tessa," he murmured huskily, slipping one hand up her back and pulling her closer so that he could kiss her throat. "I could stay like this forever."

Heat flashed through her at the touch of his lips, at his words. She felt her passion soar upward, quivering on the brink of completion. When he captured her mouth, thrusting his tongue inside, the surge of passion that went through her sent her toppling over the brink. She groaned into his mouth as her body began to quake with tremors of release. The rippling clench of the muscles along her passage massaged him, milked him of his seed despite his efforts to cling to the fine edge of pleasure a little longer. He tore his mouth from hers, driving deeply, shuddering, groaning harshly as his body erupted in bliss too intense to hold inside.

As his breathing gradually returned to normal, he began to smooth her hair and stroke his hand along her back. Dipping his head, he sucked a tender bite of skin along her shoulder, running his tongue across it. "Earth woman tastes good."

Tessa smiled against his neck and sucked a love bite there. "Saitren man, too."

As the mists of passion dissipated, she began to wonder if he was uncomfortable. She stirred.

His arms tightened. "Stay. I like the way it feels when I'm inside of you."

She liked the way it felt to have him inside of her too. She subsided, content to say just as she was.

Lucien brought her flowers when he returned the following evening. Tessa managed to accept them without bursting into tears, but she was deeply touched and swamped once more with guilt.

The flowers were exotically beautiful, in colors such as she'd never seen before. Their perfume was light, but sweet.

He began to bring her some little something almost every time he went away--more clothing, flowers, strange sweets, sometimes fruit--until she could no longer pretend she didn't know that he was courting her. She just wasn't certain why he was courting her. She couldn't leave, even if she wanted to. Her uneasiness about having to face the 'punishment' he'd threatened had subsided, but not to such a degree that she had a burning desire to test him. In any case, she was far less tempted now that she knew that Lucien knew of a ship that could take her off world, or at least had had knowledge of one in the past.

Unfortunately, there didn't seem to be any way that she could broach the subject without sounding way too interested, in which case he would know instantly that her mind was still focused on escaping.

The seasons began to change, the warm days giving way to cooler ones and cold nights. Lucien built a brazier in the center of the living area, piping the smoke from the wood they burned up through the roof. They were curled up together in front of it one evening when it finally occurred to her that she might approach the subject of the ship in a round about way.

"You're a scientist?"

He stirred, staring silently at the dancing flames for a while. "I was. Not now. Now I only chop trees and search for the necessities to survive."

"But you said that it was a plague that struck Nadryl, and you had found the cure."

He shrugged. "Micro organisms, air borne--alien--part plant, part animal--they drifted here, infected the population--they leave dead worlds in their wake. The infection was massive before we even realized what was happening. The death rate was staggering. From contact to death, most didn't last two days and very soon there were not enough living to properly dispose of the dead. It killed so fast we thought, at first, that the disease would kill itself off. It didn't, but it was like nothing we had ever seen. By the time we managed to isolate it, a good fifty to sixty percent of the population was dead or dying--including the majority of those working on trying to find a vaccine. Those who were left managed to develop a vaccine, but we had no time to test it--we tested it on ourselves. When we didn't die, we tried to get it to others, but the entire infrastructure of Heillius had collapsed by that time. We reached a few, but very few."

Tessa was sorry she'd brought it up. In retrospect, she saw that it had been a totally asinine thing to do, to make him dredge up his nightmare past only because she'd hoped it might lead the conversation toward the information she wanted. "I'm so sorry. I shouldn't have brought it up. I know it must be painful for you to talk about."

His arms tightened briefly. "No. It's past time to let it go. That was many years ago now--when I was too young to understand that there is a vast difference between living--and merely existing."

Tessa moved restlessly, uncomfortable with the turn

of his thoughts. "It's the same thing."

"No. I existed before. Existing is living day to day, with no future. Living is having tomorrow to look forward to."

He was silent for a time, stroking his hand almost idly along her belly. Finally, he settled his palm over it. "I would like to put my baby here--to watch it grow," he said quietly.

As quietly as he said it, the words sent a jolt of shock through her that leached her of color and warmth, demolishing her mind into a chaotic quagmire of conflicting thoughts and emotions. The first thought to flash through her mind was to wonder if her birth control was still effective, the second that unauthorized pregnancies carried a fine or jail time or both. The third thought to shoot through her mind was the realization that she would be bound to Lucien forever if she became pregnant with his child and it would only make an already difficult situation more so. Beyond that came the fear that her birth control had failed and she might already be pregnant, and the anxiety of whether or not such a pregnancy was even possible between two beings so radically different.

She never managed to fully grasp even one thought, however, before another replaced it. She was so deeply in the grips of her shock that she might not have even noticed Lucien's departure at all except for the fact that she began shivering in reaction when his warmth left her. She glanced toward him as he moved away, but she didn't really see him. Her mind was too busy inventing disturbing thoughts to allow room for anything else.

Days passed in a total fog of fear and confusion for

her. When she finally emerged sufficiently to begin to notice her surroundings once more, she realized, distantly, that Lucien seemed withdrawn. She was far more relieved than curious, however, thinking only about how difficult it was to try to behave with any normalcy, and certainly to interact, when she could not seem to sort her emotions.

The thing that scared her the most, she thought, was that, once he'd put the idea in her head, it became a thing she wanted desperately. The part of her mind that was still capable of rational thought tried to reason with the insane desire, but it grew all the same, tempting her to throw caution and reason to the wind.

She finally yielded to the mindless, fear driven urge, to simply escape so that she didn't have to make a decision she couldn't for the life of her make with even a speck of reason.

She managed to make it over the wall and half way back to the city before Lucien caught up to her.

Chapter Fourteen

Tessa was absolutely certain she had never seen Lucien in such a towering rage. One look at the expression on his face was sufficient to strike terror straight down to her toes and root her to the ground as if she'd been petrified and turned to stone. The moment he took a step toward her, however, adrenaline lent wings to her feet and they nearly outran her beating a retreat.

Unfortunately, Lucien could run at least twice as fast as she could, and even if he couldn't run her down, he had only to fly and she was done for. He didn't even attempt to run her down. He swooped down upon her from the sky like a giant bird of prey and snatched her off her feet. She fought so ferociously to free herself that he almost dropped her twice. Tangling his fingers in her hair, he arched her head back until her lips parted of their own accord. When he covered her mouth with his own, she knew she was lost.

An overwhelming rush of lassitude filled her as he summoned her will into his keeping with the stroke of his tongue. Oblivion swept up to meet her.

When she regained consciousness, she was tied to the bed and Lucien was standing over her. Her gaze was caught instantly by his cock, jutting from his belly like a lance. Swallowing with an effort, she dragged her gaze upward to his face. "I'm sorry," she said hoarsely. "I … I wasn't thinking. I panicked."

His face hardened. He leaned over her, bracing himself on his palms. "I do not have to ask for what I want," he said between clenched teeth. "I can take it."

He clamped his mouth over hers when she opened it to protest. With a sense of despair, she felt herself sinking, floating, drifting beyond herself as he possessed her angrily, enthralling her with his drugging kiss.

He scarcely allowed her tense muscles time to adjust to the girth of his cock, impaling her body to her core with the same anger that he had thrust his tongue into her mouth, but if anything the fine pain as he withdrew and drove into her again and again, lifting her from the bed with the force of his thrusts only seemed to send her body higher and faster toward that pinnacle of pleasure she knew he would not allow her to breach. Within moments, she was gasping for breath, moaning almost incessantly. He held her there, never allowing her to descend more than a hair's breadth from the peak before he'd forced her to the edge once more.

Her body began to burn for release, to scream for it, but he would neither allow her surcease or cease tormenting her. Each time he withdrew from her completely and relief would filter through the heated haze of passion with the thought that he would allow her to rest, that her body would at least be able to cool, he would begin all over again.

He didn't stop until her body reached such a degree of overload that she simply passed out.

He allowed her to rest just long enough for her body to cool and her mind to become crystal clear, so that she knew what he meant to do to her again. She searched his face, in the thin hope that his some of his anger, at least, had burned itself out, but saw no sign of it. She didn't even try to protest when he submerged her once more in the opium of desire, but her body protested the aggressiveness of his first thrust, clenching painfully around his engorged cock, before it spasmed with pleasure and flooded her passage with the lubrication that made each successive driving thrust easier for him.

Her body, completely under his control, shot toward climax the moment he rammed his cock into her and stayed there, setting her on fire with need. The second time, it took her body far longer to reach the point where it could take no more stimulation and to release her into oblivion.

Her legs were so weak and shaky that he had to half carry her when he untied her restraints and allowed her to attend her needs. Her only thought when she climbed into the shower was to cool the fire in her body and buy a little more time. She didn't realize until he'd led her to the bed once more and bound her that she'd only succeeded in adding to misery.

When he drove his cock into her again, her sex quivered in protest and then fire shot through her icy skin. She tried to focus her mind on something else, anything, but each savage caress of her sensitive inner flesh brought her mind to focus on the almost electric jolts of pleasure that radiated through her.

By the time he allowed her to rest again, her body had reached a point where it would no longer cool significantly, hovering near release even when he ceased to touch her. She noticed, vaguely, that it was dark, but she couldn't recall whether the passage of time meant a full day had passed or not.

He'd said four days if she ran again.

She didn't think she could make it through four, but she began to focus on the second day from the last time. He'd tormented her for a full day, withholding release, but he'd brought her to climax over and over on the second--which was almost as tortuous but something to look forward to--the end of finding no surcease, the end of the 'punishment'.

There didn't seem to be an end. The room grew light, then dark again and the pleasure began to be more pain than pleasure. By the second day--the third?--she began to beg him for release. She felt fevered, delirious and she could no longer tell whether it was the drug or if she really was out of her mind with fever.

When he finally gave in to her pleas and brought her to fulfillment, she wept.

The sun was shining in the room when she woke. Still dazed, she stared up at Lucien hopelessly, feeling tears leak from her eyes and run down her temples into her hair. When he leaned over her, hopeless anger filtered through her. "I wish I had let you die," she whispered hoarsely.

He swallowed convulsively, his face twisting in pain. "It would have been far kinder than what you did to me, Tessa," he said hoarsely. "*You* are the difference between living and only existing. You gave me hope, and then you took it from me."

When she woke again, Lucien was gone, and so too was the collar and chain that had bound her.

Chapter Fifteen

Something had changed radically, but Tessa was too sore and ill to care at first. After two days of determined effort, she regained her strength and worked most of the soreness from her muscles.

She saw very little of Lucien. She was glad at first, knowing he was still angry. He'd been angry for days afterward the first time. When he was there, he refused to meet her gaze. Mostly he simply stood by the window, staring out.

What began to truly disturb her, however, was that he no longer slept with her. As little as she wanted to remember her flight and the results of it, she began trying to search her memory for the reason he'd become so cold and distant. Vaguely, she remembered saying something hateful to him when she'd been half out of her mind.

A coldness washed over her when she did remember, but he had to know that she'd hardly known where she was or what she was saying, that she'd only said it in anger. She hadn't meant it.

Indignation warred for a time with remorse. He hadn't apologized for tormenting her. Why should she apologize for being nasty back?

Because it was bothering her conscience? Because she felt sick with remorse?

He merely stared at her when she apologized however.

"I didn't mean it. I really didn't. I was just angry."

He looked away, staring out the window. "If I had not tried so hard to save them, I would have died with my people," he said tiredly, almost absently. "It seems a poor reward for the effort--my life for everyone else's--but I suppose it's the penalty for not doing enough fast enough. The only thing worse than losing everyone that matters to you is finding there's no one left even to give you solace."

Tears stung her eyes. How could she have been so blind that she couldn't see how shattered he was by all he'd lost? She'd known that he grieved so deeply that he couldn't bear to speak of it, and yet he'd seemed so strong, so capable, she'd dismissed the pain she'd seen in him, thinking him beyond it. "But--they're not all gone. There are others out there."

"Yes. We are scattered like leaves in the wind."

He was silent for a while. Tessa had just decided that he'd gone back to ignoring her when he spoke again. "You are better. Tomorrow, I will take you home."

Tessa's heart skipped several beats. "To Earth?"

He nodded, but he didn't turn to look at her. "Yes. To Earth. To your people."

Tessa felt like bursting into tears. She just couldn't decide whether it was from relief, that she would actually see her home world again, or if it was because she'd no sooner been handed what she'd thought she wanted than she realized it wasn't the thing she most desired.

Confusion filled her. She had been so afraid that she would never see familiar faces and places again that she'd thought of little else besides the loss of something she hadn't even realized was dear to her heart. She had not once considered when she had left Earth that she might not see it again. Maybe that was why she'd been so willing to go? Because she'd been so certain that she could go back if she wanted to.

Maybe it wasn't Earth she wanted so much as the choice? The knowledge that she could go if she wanted to?

She shook that thought off. Nadryl was a dying world--giving up its last gasp, not the world so much as the people of its world, but still not a place, surely, that any sane person would choose unless it was home? Certainly no woman in her right mind would choose such a place to bear her children.

A coldness swept through her at that thought, but it wasn't the memory of the results of her panicked flight.

Lucien had mentioned having a baby with her. She couldn't remember what she'd said or what she'd done. Had she said or done anything at all? Was that why he had become so withdrawn?

She must have said no. That must be why he'd decided to take her home.

She couldn't remember saying anything, though. Her mind was nearly as blank on that incident as when she was so worn out from being 'punished' that she couldn't even think.

She pushed it from her mind. She didn't want to think about it. She didn't want to be torn. She just wanted to go home, where it was safe--or safer--where nobody had wings or looked at her in such a way that she wanted to die.

They left the mansion at sunrise, heading northward. When they'd reached the tree line, Lucien paused, turning to study the building. Tessa glanced uneasily from him to the mansion and back again, but he turned without a word after a few moments and moved on. Within a half an hour, they came upon a long, low building. Tessa stared at it in surprise as they approached it, realizing that it was on the grounds of the mansion. It didn't look like a hanger.

"What is this place?"

"My lab."

Tessa glanced at him sharply. His lab. She turned to glance back in the direction from which they'd come, staring at the small wedge of building that she could see through the trees. His home. He'd brought her home.

Something painful tightened in her chest.

She turned back to him when she heard the scrape of metal against metal and realized he'd brought the key to unlock it.

It was dim in the interior, but enough light filtered through the row of small windows near the ceiling to see that dust covered everything in a thick layer. It didn't look as if he'd been in it in years.

She couldn't help but wonder what his lab had to do with taking her home, but maybe he'd decided he needed something from it before they went?

He led her through what looked like the main lab down a short corridor to a flight of stairs that led up. Tessa glanced around in confusion. She didn't remember the building looking as if it had had two floors. After a moment, she followed him. He was waiting for her at the top. When she came even with him, he opened the door.

Tessa felt her stomach drop as she stared into the

absolute blackness. "What is it?"

"A corridor through space." He shrugged. "A dimension jump. I'm not entirely certain except that it joins many worlds to this one."

Tessa blinked, turning to stare at him. "I don't think I understand."

His lips twisted wryly. "We never conquered space travel. We were far too busy killing each other. We found the path to the stars and we used it."

Tessa's heart was pounding in her ears so loudly she could scarcely hear. "But--how do you know where you'll come out?"

"We mapped them long ago. If my people have traveled to your world before, then there is a corridor to reach it."

"I don't think I really want to do this," Tessa said uneasily. In fact, she knew she didn't. The urge was still strong to go home, but there had been a stronger one to stay from the moment she'd learned that she was free to make the choice--and, even if it were not for that, this ... nothingness into the unknown terrified her.

He frowned. "I know you have no reason to trust me, Tessa, but I would not allow harm to come to you." He stepped closer, pulling her shivering body tightly against his. "Breathe deeply."

She thought that she'd hyperventilated and lost consciousness. One moment she was gasping, the next, total blackness surrounded her. She couldn't see anything at all, but she could feel Lucien's arms around her. She felt for his chest, skated her palms upward and wrapped them tightly around his neck. Minutes passed. Abruptly, they tumbled out into a softer blackness and warmth. When Tessa opened her eyes, she saw that she was staring at a night sky. A ring of moons hovered in the sky above them.

Helping her to her feet, Lucien led her to the next gateway. It was like being sucked through a wind tunnel. Air surrounded them, as if the gateways funneled air from one point to the next, like a natural drain, but it moved so swiftly, or they moved so swiftly, it was almost impossible to drag in a breath once they'd stepped inside one of the corridors. She had to fight down panic when they made the first three jumps, certain she would suffocate before they were shot from it. Her fear lessened after a while, but it never completely left her.

When she opened her eyes at last and saw the moon and constellations of Earth, disbelief was uppermost in her mind. "It's Earth," she said disbelievingly. How could this be here when we never found it?"

"You are certain?" Lucien asked, looking around.

At the strange note in his voice, Tessa looked around, as well. "It's a desert."

His brows rose. "It is a dead land."

She glanced at him. "Not as dead as it looks, actually … but certainly not a fertile area … and not a place I'm familiar with."

He studied her for a long moment. "I can take you to a place you know. I do not like to leave you in a desolate land such as this."

Tessa's heart seemed to trip over itself, but it wasn't fear for herself. She hadn't realized that he had only meant to bring her and leave.

She supposed she should have. She just hadn't thought beyond getting home.

It scared her, though, to think of him leaving her.

Swallowing with an effort, she moved toward him. "Yes, please."

It was almost as scary flying with him as it had been the first time. More accurately, she supposed, initially, it was just as frightening, but they traveled days before they left the desert and she found she couldn't sustain fear that long. They'd brought no supplies to sustain them. She supposed she should have realized when Lucien hadn't that he expected to return immediately, but she hadn't been thinking very clearly about anything for a while.

They came at last to a small town beyond the desert, but the moment they were spotted the inhabitants fled in terror, babbling about demons and racing to grab weapons.

They moved on quickly, but as much as it had unnerved her, Tessa was also indignant. "They are ignorant, superstitious people. I don't know what country this is, but they are backwards."

Lucien gave her a look. "I think you were right. My people came here before."

She slipped back into the town alone and took supplies for them. Lucien was very much against it, but they'd had no food or water in two days. They had to have them and, as noticeable as she was among the dark skinned people, she was still far less noticeable than he was.

Tessa saw the first indication that something was terribly wrong when they came to a small city on the fourth day. The streets were virtually deserted except for the looters running from building to building. "Something is happening here. This isn't right."

Two days later they at last reached an area that was familiar. "A domed city! This is my land--my country."

She frowned, though, as they drew nearer, trying to figure out what didn't seem right. After a few minutes, she realized that it was dusk and she could only see a sprinkling of lights here and there. "Must be a blackout," she murmured, more to herself than to Lucien.

Lucien frowned. "We will look from the dome before we try to enter the city."

"I'm sure that's all it is."

It wasn't. No matter where they looked down at the city, they saw much the same as they'd seen in the other city--virtually deserted streets and looters.

"It's the plague," Lucien said quietly.

Tessa glanced at him sharply. "You don't know that!"

He looked at her steadily. "Denial will only mean that more will die. Trust me. I know what the beginning of the end looks like."

Tessa looked down at the city again, feeling horror roll over her. "You're certain?"

"Yes."

"Could you … can you produce the cure here, do you think?"

"If I had a lab--yes."

Tessa bit her lip, thinking. "The best place to go would be the CDC--they'd have everything you could possibly need besides the means to distribute it quickly once it's developed, but it's still a long way from here."

"How far?"

She made a wry gesture. "I'm not completely sure of where we are--but at least as far as we've already come--East of here."

It took them three days to reach Atlanta. By that time, even Tessa was no longer in any doubt that Lucien was right. It was the same, or worse, in every city they passed.

She had not expected to witness first hand what had happened on Lucien's world and she was sick with the fear that Earth would suffer the same fate.

Lucien refused to go anywhere near any of the populated areas, which made it difficult to find supplies. Despite the fact that Atlanta looked to be in the same state of turmoil as every other city they'd seen, Tessa was infinitely relieved when they saw the gleam of the city dome in the distance. They had no idea how long the disease had been ravaging the population, but it had not taken much more than a month to wipe out half of Nardyl's population. The domed cities might make it that much easier for the plague to spread--the domes had obviously failed to prevent the infection to start with.

They were refused entrance to the city. The guards scarcely even looked at Tessa. Their gazes were fastened with hostility on Lucien. "We have to get to the CDC. He's a scientist. He can develop a cure for the disease."

The guards exchanged a look. "There is no disease. The city is rioting. We're under martial law. No one goes in or out without clearance."

"Then send someone to get clearance! I'm Dr. Tessa Bergin. I left here in '75 with the expedition to explore a new world we'd discovered in the Claxton Galaxy.

Dr. Henry Boyd from the CDC went with us. Someone there must remember him."

They were detained and placed in confinement. Tessa paced the ten foot by ten foot room restlessly. She glanced at Lucien uncomfortably from time to time, but he didn't seem either surprised or greatly perturbed by their reception.

He'd expected it. He'd told her that he had tried to help others and each time he'd been met with distrust and hostility.

As hours passed and they saw no one, she began to worry that they'd been locked away and forgotten. Finally, when she'd begun to think that she might as well try to find a comfortable spot to sleep, the door was opened. A half dozen guards surged through. Falling upon Lucien, they dragged him from the bench where he sat and began beating him with fists and clubs when he tried to defend himself. She was so stunned she couldn't even move for several moments, but when she finally shook her shock off and tried to help, she was thrown to the floor and handcuffed, as well.

"What's going on here? Is everybody mad?"

They ignored her questions, hauling her to her feet and escorting her from the room. When she looked back, she saw that Lucien was being dragged. He was bleeding from a cut beside his eye. They were separated at the flight deck. She was placed in one vehicle and Lucien in another. Terror seized her as she watched them taking Lucien away. "Where are we being taken?" she demanded.

The cop in the front of the cruiser threw a scowl in her direction. "If you'll behave yourself, we'll take you to the CDC. Anymore disorderly conduct, and we'll lock you up for twenty four hours."

Rage and fear surged through Tessa, but she tamped it. It wasn't going to do her or Lucien any good if both of them were thrown into jail.

Her greeting at the CDC was cold, stiff and laced with obvious suspicion. She explained the situation to the director for hours. Finally, the director sent for a serologist and Tessa had to explain once more. When she'd finished, the two simply exchanged suspicious glances.

"What is it with you people, anyway!" Tessa demanded finally. "I've explained this for hours. People are dying out there and there are only going to be more tomorrow and more the day after that."

The director fixed her with a cold glance. "The problem is Dr. Tessa Bergin was reported missing and presumed dead by the members of the *Meadowlark* expedition. Dr. Henry Boyd, along with five other scientists, was also reported as a casualty. And yet, here you are."

"Don't tell me you didn't do a damned retina scan when I came through that door, because I damn well know better. You *know* I am who I say I am."

"Yes. We just don't know why, or how, you managed to get here. The *Meadowlark* is only halfway back."

"I explained that, too, and I don't see what it's got to do with this anyway. If you'd spoken to Lucien instead of having him locked up like a criminal, he could explain it far better than I can. I'm just an anthropologist."

The director exchanged a look with the serologist. "The main problem we're having is the coincidence between what happened on PIM9162 and what's happening here, and the fact that one of those who might be responsible just happens to be here."

Tessa stared at the woman in disbelief. "You think he had something to do with this? We didn't even know it was here until we got here last week. He only came to bring me home."

"Members of the Meadowlark were attacked without provocation and killed. Obviously, this is a race hostile to us. If they have the capability to travel as you say, how are we to know he didn't bring it here before?"

"*Why* would he do that? What possible motive do you think he'd have to destroy our world?"

"There seem to be strong indications that the people of his world acted aggressively toward ours long ago. We've reviewed the reports from the *Meadowlark*. What would their motive have been then, other than an act of brutality purely for the sake of dominating another species?"

Tessa ground her teeth in frustration, glaring at the woman. Finally, she stalked to the woman's desk and slammed her palms down on the edge. "*Your* ancestors killed millions of people, trying to wipe out an entire race." She turned and pointed at the serologist. "Your ancestors systematically tortured and killed thousands upon thousands of people--only to claim more land. If there's one single race on this entire planet than can claim never to have been violent and aggressive--they probably died out a long time ago. You don't expect to be judged on something you had nothing to do with. How can you judge him?"

"The attack on the crew from the Meadowlark wasn't thousands of years ago."

"And not only did Lucien have nothing to do with it, but it was *not* an act of aggression. You seem to forget, we didn't belong there. It's *their* world. And it was an act of survival. They had no way of knowing whether or not we were more of those who'd already come to scavenge what little they had left. They had a *right* to defend their territory. If it was us, you know damn well we would've shot them down and asked questions later.

"Lucien has offered to help. He's the only one who can help us and if you don't do something, our world is going to look like his, or worse."

"How do we even know if he *can* help?" the serologist asked after a moment.

Tessa turned to look at him. "He's alive. Ninety percent of the population of Nadryl died. Either he knows just as he says he does, or he's naturally immune--in either case, he's the only hope we've got."

They brought him in chains, under guard. Tessa felt like weeping when she saw him, but they wouldn't allow her to go any where near him and from the glance he sent her way she realized she wasn't welcome anyway. To her horror, instead of asking for his help, they chained him to a gurney and took his blood to test it.

The cold certainty began to creep into her mind that they were fully capable of bleeding him dry if they saw he had what they needed, or turning him over to some other agency for studies if they thought they could manufacture the cure fast enough that they didn't need him. The former seemed the most likely scenario, however, since time was something they didn't have.

Chapter Sixteen

The entire building was in chaos by the time they brought Lucien in. The plague was escalating and no one had time for anything beyond dashing from station to station in a frantic effort to run tests to isolate the agent that was killing everyone and find something to stop it.

Once Lucien was strapped to the bed, he was locked into the room and a single guard left to watch the door.

Turning away resolutely, Tessa ducked into the first supply room and grabbed a lab coat. From there she measured the distance to the roof of the building, noting that it took no more than ten minutes to reach it even at only a brisk walk--at a run, if they needed to, they could probably make it in half that time. The parking lot was full. She checked vehicle after vehicle, however, before she found an older model with defective security that she was able to breach.

She would've preferred something newer and faster, but it was fully charged and had a thousand mile radius. If they managed to get away without being noticed they wouldn't need speed and the older vehicle wouldn't be noticed as readily.

It would have to do. Whether her logic was actually reasonable or inspired by hope, they didn't have any options.

There was no way she was going to allow anything to happen to Lucien if she could do anything to prevent it.

Retracing her steps, she ducked into the supply room again, found a larger men's lab coat and grabbed a handful of specimen knives. The blades were barely long enough to cause a painful scratch, but there was nothing else that even resembled a weapon.

It wasn't likely she could get the guard's weapon.

She waited almost an hour just around the corner from Lucien's room, hoping the guard would be called away for something, or leave on his own. She'd almost given up hope and begun trying to think of something she could do to distract him when a call came over the inner com unit for all security officers to report to the lobby to control a mob. The moment the guard stepped into the elevator, Tessa strode briskly to the room. The door was locked. Gritting her teeth in vexation, she dug a knife from her pocket and began working frantically at the lock.

She was sweating with fear of discovery before she managed to get it open. Closing it quietly behind her, she rushed over to the gurney. Lucien, to her relief, was awake and alert.

"We have to get out of here," she whispered.

Her hands were shaking so badly she thought she'd never manage to slip the restraints off of him. When she finally managed to free one hand, however, he began working on the other wrist restraint and she moved to his ankles.

When he was free, she helped him to pull the lab coat on.

There was no hiding the damned wings. Even closed tightly against his back, the top 'knuckle' pushed through the collar of the coat. Beyond the cap and mask she'd brought to cover his face and the horns, there was nothing more she could do to help disguise him, however.

She hoped the chaos would help them to escape.

To her relief, no one so much as glanced at them as they hurried down the corridor and up the stairs to the roof. Directing Lucien to the vehicle she'd found, she climbed into the pilot's seat and secured her safety straps.

She had trouble getting the vehicle started. She tried not to think of it as a very bad sign. When she finally managed to get it going, she turned to look at Lucien. "We can't get out through the gates. We'd run into the same problem going out as had when we came in."

His brows rose questioningly. "Is there another way?"

Tessa shrugged. "Straight through the dome."

Lucien looked around at the vehicle. "Will this go through?"

Tessa smiled with an effort. "We're about to find out."

Revving the engine, she left the roof and headed straight through town, ignoring the designated flight paths. There was little traffic on any of them, but she suspected any traffic stops would be set up for the main thoroughfares. In point of fact, the police had their hands full with the looters and rioting. They passed straight through the heart of the city without so much as a challenge.

"They have developed the serum?"

"They drew blood. They've got what they need. I didn't feel like waiting around to see if they would decide to feel better about the two of us once they had isolated the antibodies."

"You have not been inoculated?"

"I couldn't wait for that, either," Tessa said grimly. She tensed as she saw the doom looming before them. "Assuming we make it through, where is the gateway back?"

"It would be in the same area."

She nodded, but she was focused on lining the vehicle up with the widest space. The glass, she knew, would be thinnest near the apex of the dome because of the weight. The uppermost 'windows' were reinforced with steel mesh, however. She chose the first row below that cap line. She would've far preferred to try something lower, in the event that they made it through but the vehicle was too smashed up to continue, or to land, but she was fairly certain 'snowball's chance in hell' fairly accurately summed their chances up there.

They would never have made it through the check points elsewhere, however.

She swallowed the lump of fear in her throat. "Assuming we make it through ... you should be ready to bail in case this thing can't fly afterwards."

He nodded, glancing at her sharply. "What is the chance we'll make it through?"

Tessa smiled wryly. "Unfortunately, I'm neither a structural engineer nor a mathematician--no good at calculating the odds, or all that certain I've picked the right spot. On the good side--these vehicles use solid fuel, so they hardly ever blow up, and it has crash protection--if it still works."

She also, unfortunately, had no idea of whether speed would help or not. She decided not to hit it at full throttle, however. A slower speed might make it anyway, and it would definitely make it easier to aim the vehicle directly at the opening and lessen the risk of hitting the steel beams that surrounded the specially designed glass.

When they slammed into it, Tessa heard breaking glass, crunching metal, the blast preceding the escape of the crash foam, and then nothing. Time virtually stood still, everything moving in slow motion around her. Even she moved as if she was in a dream, unable to do more than float, unable to hear, seeing images in abrupt, disjointed clips.

As abruptly as time had ceased, it kicked back in at high velocity. Every warning alarm on the vehicle was sounding at one time. She couldn't see past the protective foam in front of her, but the downward spiral of the vehicle was unmistakable. They'd crashed through, she thought, and were nose diving--probably because she'd lost her grip on the controls as much as anything done to the vehicle. She fought to pull it up and level it out, expecting to become a smear in the bottom of a crater any second or slam into the remains of one of the many abandoned buildings beyond the dome.

The moment she'd managed to level the vehicle, she began clawing at the foam to clear a spot large enough see. Even so, she could barely see well enough to negotiate a path through the derelict buildings. As soon as she found a space large enough to land, she dropped the personal craft to the ground long enough to clear the windows.

The vehicle was, naturally enough, running badly, but it was still going. When they were airborne once more, she managed to chart a direct course with the computer--or at least as direct as she could given that she wasn't exactly certain of the name of the first town they'd come to. Setting it at top speed, which was about half what it should have been able to perform, she slumped wearily in her seat.

"We should not have left. They will need help to develop the serum quickly."

Tessa sighed, realizing now that they seemed to have the worst behind them that she was so tired and achy all she wanted to do was to find a cool place to sleep. "The *Meadowlark* reported the attacks on the landers. They wouldn't listen. I tried." She was silent for several moments. "If I had even suspected the reception we would get I'm not so sure I would've asked you to go in the first place."

"You did not need to ask. I would still have gone."

She shook her head. It produced a disorienting dizziness, and she closed her eyes for a moment until it passed. "You're right. It had to be done. I'm just sorry they hurt you."

"I will live."

Setting the vehicle on auto pilot, she waited to make certain the auto pilot was working properly and finally turned to Lucien. "I'm going back with you."

He glanced at her sharply and finally nodded. "You should have the vaccine. It will be quicker to return to my lab than to wait until they have enough to go around."

Tessa bit her lip but decided to let the subject drop for the moment. She had done and said too many terrible things to have much hope that Lucien would listen to her. She at least wanted to wait to try to talk to him when they could actually talk without fear of interruption. The vehicle seemed to be holding its own, but it was anybody's guess whether it would actually make it to their destination.

There'd been no signs of pursuit, but that didn't mean that there wouldn't be. Ordinarily, she would've considered it enough that they'd gotten away clean. But these weren't ordinary times. Once the CDC discovered she'd absconded with their lab rat, who just happened to be carrying the antibodies they needed to reproduce a lot of vaccine very quickly, they weren't just likely to send the military after them. It was almost a foregone conclusion. Once they'd cleared land, however, she had set the craft to skim the surface of the gulf, which she hoped would make them harder to track.

The vehicle was moving at a snail's pace, but they were outside U.S. territorial waters--not that she deluded herself into thinking that would do them any good if the military was sent to fetch them--and they were taking a straight shot to the Mexican desert, which cut miles off their route.

She thought it was probably unlikely given the condition of the craft even before she'd smashed it all to hell going through the dome, but she hoped they could make it to the Mexican coast before the vehicle tapped out.

They didn't, but they were only a few miles out and could see the lights along the coast when the vehicle began to choke and sputter and the engine finally quit altogether. As close as they were to the surface, the impact seemed to rattle every tooth in her head. The craft began to sink the moment it touched the water.

Breaking a window out, Lucien climbed on top of the sinking vehicle and helped her out.

Scooping her into his arms, Lucien launched himself into the sky and they went airborne once more, this time under his steam. Looping her arms around Lucien's neck, Tessa lay her head against his shoulder tiredly. She was so relieved that she'd managed to help Lucien get away before they managed to do any lasting harm to him that she didn't even flinch at finding herself airborne with nothing between her and the ground but his arms.

They were wonderful arms ... and he'd carried her in them across a dozen worlds.

"I'm so thirsty, Lucien. Can we stop and get water before we go home?"

Lucien glanced down at her worriedly and finally pressed his cheek to hers. "You are hot."

"I think that's why I'm so thirsty. It must be summer to be so hot even after dark."

"That must be it," he said quietly. "I will get water for you."

By the time they stopped for water, Tessa felt as if her throat was on fire. There didn't seem to be any molecule of her body that didn't hurt. She thought it must have been the crash. She'd been too flooded with adrenaline and fear to feel the effects at the time. She drank the water gratefully when Lucien brought it to her, but she couldn't seem to get enough.

"Just a little more for now," Lucien said firmly, pouring a little into his palm and smoothing it over her face. "I'll give you more later."

"I don't feel at all well, Lucien," Tessa said dizzily.

"I know, my love. You'll feel better in a little while."

She didn't, but she was almost beyond knowing or caring. She was only vaguely aware of anything going on around her. Every time they stopped, she asked Lucien if they were home.

"Not yet, love."

"Let's just rest here a while. I hurt all over. I just want to lie down."

"In a little while."

By the time they stepped from the corridor and onto Nadryl, she'd stopped asking. She roused, however, when Lucien lay her down on a cold stone floor, gasping as it sent a painful chill through her hot skin. She saw when she opened her eyes that she was lying on the floor of his lab. He bent over her, stabbing something into her arm, and she winced.

"What're you doing?"

"Drawing blood."

"Why?"

Instead of replying, he patted her cheek and moved away. He seemed to be gone for a very long time. She wasn't certain, because she thought she'd fallen asleep for a little while. She roused again when he picked her up. She discovered it took a supreme effort to loop her arms around his neck.

She sighed with relief and contentment when he finally settled her on their bed.

He was sleeping in a chair beside the bed when she woke. She lay watching him for a while, wondering why he was in the chair instead of sleeping with her, but finally decided he was still angry with her.

When she woke again, he was standing at the window.

He heard the rustle of the covers when she turned

onto her side. He turned to look at her and finally moved to the side of the bed, dropping his hand to her forehead. "The fever is gone."

"I was sick?" she said, and was startled when the words came out in a hoarse croak.

Sitting on the side of the bed, he picked up a mug of water and held it for her to drink. When she'd emptied it, she lay back. "I hope I don't look as badly as I feel, because I feel like hell."

Something flickered in his eyes. He looked way, setting the mug down carefully.

Tessa felt like biting her tongue off. As if it wasn't bad enough that everybody that had set eyes on Lucien had screamed demon at him, she just had to remind him. It wasn't the sort of slip one could fix, however. After several moments, she decided she was better off pretending she hadn't noticed. She grabbed his wrist when he would have risen. "I had the plague?"

"A mild case."

"Good thing. You gave me the vaccine?"

To her surprise, his skin darkened. She stared at him in surprise, realizing he was blushing. She hadn't even realized he *could* blush.

"Yes," he said vaguely.

She frowned, curious, but she released her grip on him. "I don't remember you giving me a shot."

He looked at her uncomfortably. "The antibodies were in my bodily fluids."

Tessa stared at him for several moments before what he was saying fully sank in. She bit her lip in amusement. "Well, it's a very good thing you were so assiduous in inoculating me," she said teasingly.

He sent her a curious look. After a moment,

amusement gleamed in his own eyes. In the next moment, however, he sobered. "I can not regret it. You would not have survived otherwise."

Chapter Seventeen

Even if Tessa hadn't been looking for an opening to approach Lucien, she couldn't have failed to notice that he was just as distant now as he had been before they'd left to make the trip to Earth. She'd thought, with everything that had happened, he might have gotten past some of his anger with her.

What she hadn't considered was that he wasn't just angry. He was hurt and he wasn't about to give her the chance to do any more damage than she already had.

When she saw he wasn't going to give her an opening to talk, she decided that, maybe, once they were intimate once more, he would come around. Unfortunately, he either had no desire for her, or he wasn't giving in to it because he suspected she would try to use it against him. Or maybe she'd convinced him that she had only tolerated him and he was too proud to approach her?

In all honesty, she knew she'd never looked worse in her life. She'd lost weight since she'd first arrived on Nardyl, and more while she was sick, and it wasn't a lovely improvement. Before she'd been on the very outer limits of what was allowed for space travel. Now, she could see her ribs and count most of them. Her skin still looked sickly, too, and her hair was limp and lifeless looking.

Small wonder he didn't have any trouble restraining himself.

It didn't look like he planned on allowing her to hang around long enough to show a great deal of improvement either. She'd only just begun to be up and about when he told her that he would take her back as soon as they were certain the danger had passed on Earth.

"How long?" she asked, feeling slightly nauseous.

"Four weeks or five. It will have run its course by then, or they will have wiped it out."

She had a month to try to court him into allowing her back 'in', or to seduce him.

Surely to god being the only female in a hundred miles or more ought to do it!

She tried everything she could think of, but it seemed the harder she tried, the more distant he got.

She would've tried running away again except that she was fairly certain he'd let her go.

She walked around the next thing to naked. He hadn't touched her in weeks. Surely, any man capable of going for two or three nights straight had to be horny as hell!

As soon as she stopped looking like she was on the verge of dying on the road, she stopped wearing anything at all.

For days, he watched her stroll around the apartment through narrowed, assessing eyes, looking like nothing so much as a cat watching its prey and trying to decide whether he was actually interested enough to pounce.

On the third day, he slammed out of the house and didn't come back until the following morning.

Chastened, Tessa went back to wearing the clothing he'd brought for her and gave up trying to reach him. It was what she deserved, and she knew it. She'd never intended to hurt him, but she'd been too self-absorbed to see that she was, which was just as bad. She hadn't even realized that anything she said or did *could* hurt him until she already had. She'd been so certain that he only saw her as a 'thing' that he'd acquired for his comfort and entertainment that she hadn't even looked to see if there was anything else until it was too late.

She couldn't lie to herself that she hadn't realized he was courting her, however. She'd known that he was. She just hadn't taken it seriously, and she hadn't wanted to become emotionally involved with someone not of her own kind.

The irony was that she'd never met anyone of her own 'kind' that she'd felt the same way about as she did Lucien. Not even close.

Maybe, deep down, she'd been afraid that even if she accepted him, none of her peers would--and they certainly hadn't. They'd done their damnedest to kill him--shunned him, beat him, locked him up and used him for a lab rat.

The odd thing was, the moment they'd treated him like that she'd hated them instead of accepting their assessment and shunning Lucien. She'd lost all sense of 'belonging' with them. If they weren't willing to really look at Lucien and see how wonderful he was, then they didn't even deserve her contempt.

She was going to hate going back. She didn't think she would ever be able to look at any of them the same way again.

Lucien was probably right, though. It was where she belonged. She supposed she hated them because she hated herself, and she hated herself because she was just like them.

It was almost ironic that one of the main reasons she'd been so reluctant to stay with Lucien on Nardyl was because it was a brutal world, a dying world--and she would be going back to a world that probably wasn't in much better shape. Even if they'd had the sense to use what Lucien had given them and acted quickly, the plague had already been rampant when she and Lucien had arrived. It had to have decimated the population.

Regardless, and even though they had refused to accept it, they were luckier than the Saitren had been. At least they'd had somebody to come to their rescue.

When she saw that she wasn't making any headway with Lucien and wasn't likely to, she decided to move to another part of his house. It didn't seem right to run him out of the place he'd made comfortable, and she figured she might as well accustom herself to rough living conditions. If things weren't as bad as she feared they would be when she got back to Earth, she'd still be ahead.

She ran into Lucien when she went back for food. She glanced at him uncertainly several times, sighing when he moved to the window. "You don't have to leave. I'm staying in another part of the house now."

He turned around in surprise. "It is more comfortable here."

She shrugged. "Yes, but you made it comfortable. You should have it. I'll be gone in a few weeks anyway."

When he only stared at her, she looked down at the food in her arms and blushed. She hadn't even asked. She'd just helped herself. "I hope it's all right if I take some--I don't know where to find any."

He frowned and finally looked away. "I brought the food for both of us. Take what you need."

"Thanks." She was still embarrassed but it was a relief that he'd been so good-natured about her bad manners. It was strange that she'd grown so accustomed to being Lucien's mate on so many levels that it had never even occurred to her that everything wasn't 'ours' when it had taken her so much longer to accept that she belonged with him on a conscious level.

She supposed the one thing that would remain constant and unchanging as long as man was around was that no matter how much they learned they were always going to be just what they were and no more, and they were never going to completely understand themselves. She certainly didn't understand herself.

Why, she wondered, did she have to learn everything the hard way? Why couldn't she have just taken Layla's advice and accepted the 'gift' of happiness and pleasure that had fallen into her lap?

Instead, she'd worked just as hard as she could to throw it away ... and now that she'd succeeded, she'd not only managed to ruin her own happiness, she'd made Lucien unhappy.

As innocuous as the encounter with Lucien had seemed, it had shaken Tessa and she dreaded another one. She rationed the food she'd taken carefully so that it would last several days before she had to make another trip. She decided that the next time, if he wasn't there, she'd taken enough for at least week.

It was winter and although it wasn't extremely cold, it was still cold. Nevertheless, she had nothing to do since she wasn't even preparing meals for two or picking up after the two of them and she decided to explore. She found a room on the first floor that was filled with all the intellectual and technical trappings of an advanced civilization that she'd been looking for since she'd arrived on Nardyl and had thought were missing.

It was filled, primarily, with books of every description and on most any subject. She thought at first, that the written language of the Saitren was too different from her own for her to read any of the books, but when she'd sat down to examine them more carefully, she realized that the formation of the letters was only a little different in most cases. Some of the letters didn't look familiar at all, but most did, and she discovered that if she pronounced the letters in the words they formed, she could understand the strange letter groupings, as well. The Saitren vocabulary included words that were familiar and words that weren't. Naturally enough, the words they'd coined to describe inventions and technology were different.

It was fascinating, actually, to compare the divergent evolution of a language that had begun as the same language, but developed by two different species on two different worlds.

There was one book lying open on a table beside a padded chair. It wasn't dusty, which meant that Lucien had probably been down here reading much of the time when she'd wondered where he'd gotten off to. The realization made her feel like a trespasser, but as anxious as she was to leave as soon as she made the discovery, she couldn't help but be curious about the book.

Without touching it, she moved around the chair until

she could see the full page illustration on one of the open pages. Her heart did a strange little double tap when she saw the picture clearly. It was a shaded line drawing of a Saitren male. Draped across one arm limply was a female--a human female. In his other hand was a sword and in the background, humans toiling under the lash of their slave masters. Holding the place it was opened to, she lifted the front half of the book to see what the title was

An Illustrated History of Saitren Conquest; The Dark Ages.

She settled the book carefully once more and left the room. She would've liked to have examined some of the electronics in the room to see if she could figure out what they were for. She would have liked to have taken a few books to study them, but she didn't want to be caught nosing around Lucien's personal belongings.

When she was finally forced to go back to forage for more food from Lucien's larder, she waited until the middle of the day. In the past, he'd always been gone most of the day, usually leaving very early and not returning until it was nearing dusk.

She was startled when she peered inside to see if he was there and found that he was ... almost as if he'd been laying in wait for her. She would've left again except that he saw her. Embarrassed, she tried to pretend she hadn't been creeping in and moved with as much unconcern as she could muster to the kitchen area, trying to ignore the fact that Lucien was watching every move she made.

To her surprise, he moved across the room to stand on the other side of the counter from her.

"You can stay here if you like," he said after several moments, his voice sounding rough with disuse.

She threw a smile in his direction, but she didn't actually make eye contact. "No. I'm fine. Thanks anyway."

He was silent for several moments, but he didn't move away. "I meant stay here--on Nadryl--with me."

Tessa's head just seemed to snap up all by itself. She stared at him with a mixture of surprise, hope, and doubt. "Something ... terrible happened on Earth?"

He frowned. "I have not returned. They had what they needed to stop the spread of the disease. I assume they were intelligent enough to make use of it. If so, conditions would be no worse there than here-- probably far better."

"Oh." She bobbed her head and then frowned. "You didn't invited me to stay because you thought it wasn't safe to go back, then?"

He shifted uncomfortably. "I thought you might want to."

She nodded, fiddling with the container of food she'd picked up. "Do you want me to?" she asked finally, forcing herself to look up at him.

Something flickered in his eyes. He swallowed audibly. "Yes."

Tessa sighed shakily. She found she couldn't maintain eye contact, though. "Do you think, maybe ... if I did stay ... do you think you might ... do you think we could get past the mistakes and ... that you could love me again?"

He was silent for so long, she finally looked at him again.

"I will always love you, Tessa," he said hoarsely. "I

never stopped. I couldn't."

Her chin developed an unstable wobble and her eyes filled with tears. He looked so disconcerted a sound that was part chuckle and part sob erupted. She covered her mouth with her hand, trying to fight the tears of relief.

He looked like he wasn't certain whether to stay or to retreat. She swallowed with an effort and moved around the counter, slipping her arms around his waist and hugging him tightly before he could decide on the latter and she lost the chance he'd given her to make things right between them. "I'm so sorry, Lucien. I didn't mean any of those awful things I said and did that hurt you. I really didn't."

He wrapped his arms around her shaking shoulders and stroked her hair. "It's all right, Tessa. It was my fault. I … demanded more than you could give and then I was angry with you when I should not have been and I did things I should not have. I know you can not help the way you feel any more than I can."

Tessa sniffed. "I can't. I tried. I tried really hard not to feel like I do. I didn't want to at all, but I just couldn't help it."

He stroked her back soothingly. "Shhh. It will be all right." After a moment, he pulled away from her and caught her hand, tugging her with him as he moved to the lounge and sat down, then pulled her onto his lap.

"If you will think about staying," he said after a while, "I will make this place more comfortable for us."

Tessa dragged in a shuddering breath, easing the tightness in her chest. "I want to stay, Lucien."

His arms tightened around her momentarily, then he

hooked a finger beneath her chin and forced her to look up at him. "You are certain?"

"I am absolutely certain," she said steadily.

When he released her chin, she caught his hand and placed it on her belly. "I want you to put your child here. I want to watch it grow."

He swallowed with an effort. "You don't have to do that, Tessa. I understand."

Tessa felt like crying all over again. "No, you don't, but I need for you to understand … or to at least try." She stroked his hand, trying to figure out how to explain it to him so that he wouldn't think she was just making something up to try to make him feel better. "The thing is, the laws where I come from--the laws on Earth are very strict about reproduction because of the population control--or they were. I would never have been allowed to have a child at all, and because I knew that, I had never considered having one, never thought about myself in that way. When you asked me, it scared me to death because all I could think about was that maybe I was already pregnant, and if I was that I could never go home.

"And I was scared because as soon as you asked me, I wanted to in the worst kind of way and I knew if I stayed with you, sooner or later I'd give in to that desire or I'd just get pregnant anyway."

He pulled her against his chest once more and began stroking her, obviously deep in thought. "This is the truth?" he asked after a long while.

"Yes, it is the truth."

He sighed, obviously still thinking it over. "It was not because you were repulsed at the idea of carrying my child?"

Tessa struggled with herself for a few moments, but she knew she had to give him the whole truth. "I was not repulsed. I was afraid. We're not the same, and I was afraid there might be problems because of it--and, to be perfectly honest the whole idea of having a baby scares me to death. It probably wouldn't scare me as badly if I had no idea what it was all about. Unfortunately, I do. I'm an anthropologist and I know how it was before we became so advanced medically--which we don't really have anymore--so I would have to go through everything my ancestors did."

He frowned at that. "I had not thought about that."

Tessa smiled wryly. "Why would you? *You* wouldn't have to go through it."

He gave her an affection squeeze. "I had not realized that I was so unreasonable. You are right. I should not have asked. It is enough that you are willing to do it for me."

Tessa sighed, striving for patience. "You still don't understand."

"No?"

"No! *I* want it. I *want* to have your baby."

His gaze flickered over her face searchingly. "Why?"

"Because I love you and I want us to create a life together."

He cupped her cheek with his palm and leaned toward her to brush his lips against hers. "You do?"

Tessa smiled against his lips. "I do."

He kissed her with a slow thoroughness that made her toes curl. He was smiling when he pulled away. "I will give you my baby today, before you change your mind again."

Tessa chuckled. "There's just one more thing."

His dark brows rose questioningly.

"If I stay, you must promise to 'punish' me at least once in a while. I'd hate to have to do something naughty just to get it."

He stared at her a long moment and started laughing. "I think the 'punishment' must have been far worse for me than you."

"Undoubtedly. For me, it was absolutely divine."

Chapter Eighteen

Tessa sighed with a mixture of contentment and vague irritation, staring down at the huge mound of her belly as Lucien rubbed it in slow circles. "I still don't know why you didn't tell me you could make a baby whenever you wanted to."

Lucien paused. "I did. I told you I would make a baby."

"I thought you meant practice."

He was grinning when she tilted her head back to look up at him. The grin vanished abruptly. He tried to look contrite, but failed, because his eyes still gleamed with amusement. "It did not occur to me that humans did not control birth."

"We do, but not naturally--unless you count not having sex at all, which isn't really controlling it."

"You mentioned birth control. I thought the women controlled it on your world."

Tessa sighed irritably. "Never mind. I'm just miserably uncomfortable." She thought about it for a little while. "I don't suppose you control the sex of the child too?"

"It will be a son. Next time, we will have a daughter for you."

Tessa slapped his knee. "Don't talk to me about next time when I haven't even finished this time!"

Lucien tightened his arms beneath her breasts and

dragged her up his belly, kissing her neck. "Pregnant humans are very short tempered."

Tessa's lips twitched. She rubbed her distended belly affectionately. "That's because infant Saitrens are such demons. Your son has been dribbling my bladder as if he thinks it's a basketball for months."

She frowned when her belly tightened again, realizing the vague ache had been getting gradually worse. "This is so strange. Feel that."

Obediently, Lucien placed his palm on her belly. "The contractions are closer."

Tessa sat up. "Contractions? It's coming? You mean I'm having it?"

"You will know when the time comes."

She discovered a few hours later that he was right. The first crippling contraction bent her double. When it eased off, she called him every foul name she could think of and told him she'd changed her mind. He frowned at her, but instead of responding, he left her. If she hadn't been in the grips of yet another contraction, she would've begged him not to go. By the time it had subsided, however, he was back, carrying a strange looking thing that looked sort of like a chair … and sort of didn't.

"What are you doing?" she gasped breathlessly.

"Making ready."

His calmness sent a sense of relief flooding through her. He, at least, seemed to know what he was doing. She watched him as he moved about collecting various things and laying them out by the chair-like thing. He placed a thick cushion beneath the contraption and then carefully spread layer after layer of clean cloths over the cushion. When he'd finished, he helped her

from the lounge and removed her skirt, then walked
her over to the 'thing'. She stared at it in confusion,
holding her belly. When the contraction had passed, he
lifted her up and settled her on the thing, placing her
knees on two narrow, padded benches that seemed to
have been made for that purpose. The back reclined
slightly, but there was no seat to speak of, only a
narrow ledge that she could perch her buttocks on.

"What is this?" she asked a little vaguely.

"A birthing chair. It will help the baby to come more
quickly."

She was all in favor of anything that would get her
through it more quickly. The only problem was, she
hurt much, much worse. He settled on his knees
slightly in front and below her and touched her sex,
examining her. She would've been embarrassed if she
hadn't been in so much pain. Apparently, he was
satisfied. He got up after only a moment. Bracing his
palms on the chair arms that she was gripping in white
knuckled fists, he leaned toward her.

She looked at him in surprise and more than a little
irritation. It was a hell of time to decide to kiss her as
far as she was concerned, but the moment his mouth
covered hers and he kissed her deeply, dizziness swept
over her. She felt weak and calm at the same time. The
pain lessened to a dull ache.

She was only vaguely aware of anything after that. It
took all of her concentration just to remain upright.
Each time she seemed to slip, he would steady her.
Each time the pain reached a level where she began to
moan, he would kiss her and take the edge off of it so
that she felt that she could bear it a little longer.

Hours seemed to pass, but she had no real concept of

time. Finally, her belly reached a point where it seemed to remain hard. Lucien began to speak softly to her, coaxingly, telling her what to do. Then, as abruptly as a switch being turned off, the pain stopped, followed by an ungodly racket. Wearily, Tessa looked down, drawn by the sound. Lucien was on his knees, holding a horrible looking red thing that was waving two arms and legs and had half its head open, exposing a vibrating tongue and tonsils. She released a sound that was half sob and half chuckle. "He is not happy to be here."

Lucien looked up at her. The look on his face scared her.

"He's all right?" she asked fearfully.

He swallowed. "He is beautiful."

Relief flooded her. "He has everything he's supposed to have?"

He chuckled. "Yes. Everything."

He lay the squalling infant down after a few moments, watching him and then finally tied a cord tightly around the umbilical cord and cut it. When he'd finished, he rose and moved to her, gently kneading her stomach. Finally, he brought water and very gently cleaned the blood from her. When he'd bathed her off, he scooped her up and carried her to the bed, settling her against the pillows. She turned her head, watching him as he very carefully bathed the baby and finally wrapped him in one of the clean cloths he'd brought for that purpose. Cuddling the infant close to his chest, he brought it to her and settled it in her arms.

She rolled onto her side, settling the baby on the bed and unwrapping it so that she could look at it. He had ceased crying when Lucien cuddled him. She stroked his soft cheek, and he opened his eyes a sliver, squinting at her. He was so ugly she didn't know whether to laugh or cry, but he was hers--and Lucien's. She wrapped him again and cradled him against her breast when he began to whimper again. The moment he felt her breast against his cheek, he opened his mouth and began searching ... for something.

Lucien settled on the bed beside her. Without a word, he pulled her top aside and guided her nipple to the baby's questing mouth. He latched onto it instantly, balling his hands into fists on either side of his mouth and sucking frantically.

A strange sensation went through Tessa as she watched him. Finally, she lifted her head and looked at Lucien. "How did you know that was what he wanted?"

Instead of answering, he stroked her cheek and then leaned down to kiss her. When he sat back, she smiled up at him. "I'm not sure I've ever appreciated you as much as you deserve ... but I can't tell you how glad I am that you came for me that day when I landed here."

He caressed her cheek. "It was the best thing that ever happened to me. One day, I will have to find this friend of yours, Layla, and thank her for bringing you to me."

Tessa sighed. "I hope that she's as happy as I am, but I don't think it's possible."

"She might be."

Tessa shook her head. "She couldn't be ... because I have you ... and this ugly little fellow here. What should we call him, do you think?"

"Lucifer?"

Tessa chuckled.

Lucien looked a little offended. "It was my father's name."

Tessa bit her lip. "I absolutely adore you! It's perfect."

The End

Printed in the United States
36122LVS00002B/121-123